Libe

THE SANDS OF TIME

Peacock Publishing Ltd

1997

The Sands of Time

Published by Peacock Publishing Ltd
3, St. Mary's Street
Worcester WR1 1HA, England

ISBN 0-9525404-3-6

Cover design: Excalibur Graphics 1997

British Library cataloguing-in-print data has been applied for.

Typeset in New Century Schoolbook 10pt.

Printed in Malta by Interprint Ltd.

CHAPTER 1

The man in the black car glanced cursorily at his watch. There was so much to do. But he had to put up with it. He'd been the only one available to meet her.

Rik Fenton hoped Professor Adams's daughter wasn't going to disrupt the work on site too much. Probably not, if she took after her father. He had learned a few things about Pippa from his boss and he was slightly curious. He'd also heard she was sweet on Mike Nash. *That* he didn't like.

Who was going to warn her about the bloke? Rik certainly couldn't. Anyway, Pippa Adams was a psychologist by profession, so she ought to have her wits about her.

Rik Fenton ran his fingers through his thick, black hair, which was full of sand as usual. He yawned. No plane he'd been sent to meet at Heliopolis had ever been on time. It looked like this was going to be another.

He glanced at his watch again and grimaced. Then, deciding there was nothing he could do about it, he reclined the seat of the dusty Mercedes and closed his eyes thankfully. Yawning again, he stretched his long legs out as far as he could and settled down to wait for his passenger. . .

Through the shimmer of the heat haze and the press of a thousand, thronging white-clad bodies, intent on the business of coming in or getting away from Cairo Airport, the girl stood out. Her long, blonde hair flowed to waist level like a silken sheet over her shoulders. She held her head proudly erect like a model does and, indeed, her figure, clad in an expensive light safari suit, had model proportions.

Pippa shaded her eyes with her hand, then turned as the porter set down her luggage. She gave him a tip and the man salaamed and backed away. She felt uneasy instead of excited at being in Cairo at last and seeing Dad and Mike again. She shook her head at the taxi drivers, who cruised past hopefully, then she looked at her watch. It wasn't like Dad not to be there, especially when they hadn't seen each other for so long. Uneasiness welled up and gave her a shivery feeling.

She realised that part of her apprehension was because it was going to be her father, not Mike, who was coming to pick her up from the airport. It should have been Mike, she knew that, but he'd told her on the telephone that he wouldn't have the time. She stood there uncomfortable and parched, not daring to move to the kiosk for a drink in case she missed her father.

Just as she was wondering what to do next, a dusty, black Mercedes pulled into the kerb. The driver was out and round in a moment. At first she thought he was an Egyptian; his tan was deep and he had the alert, piercing look which characterised the race, but his features were too strong and his manner forceful.

"Miss Adams." He held out a tanned hand.

Pippa didn't recognise his face. She hesitated and his hand dropped.

"It's okay. No need to be suspicious. I'm Rik Fenton."
She might have known. He was just as she had imagined.
"Have you been here long?"

"Mr. Fenton," she said, extending her hand. He took it
this time. "No, the plane was late. Where's Dad?" she
said, hoping it didn't sound too ungrateful.

"I'm sorry. He was very busy and I offered. Unfortunately, I fell asleep over there in the car park," Rik Fenton
said truthfully.

"Dad was busy? And you fell asleep?" Pippa knew her
face said all the rest.

"Yes, he and Mike have broken through the third level
and I was the only one to be spared. We've had a few
rough nights."

"You don't have to explain, Mr. Fenton. I know how
important my father's work is and how it tends to take
over."

"Call me Rik, please. And your Dad is a brilliant
archaeologist."

"Thank you," she said, looking down at the luggage.
He opened the car door for her. "Shall I help you with all
this?"

"No, I'll do it," he said abruptly as he motioned her into
the front seat, closing the door as she sat down. She stayed,
watching his dark head through the driving mirror. He
yawned several times.

Her father's letters had been full of Rik Fenton. He had
written a marvellous paper on *The Pharaoh Mentuhotep
of the Eleventh Dynasty* and, according to her father,
practically everyone in the whole of the archaeological
world had admired it. Dad had said he'd been lucky to get
Fenton on the team and now he was out at the site, things
had really started to move.

Mike had thought differently. At least he hadn't said so directly, but he had implied that Rik Fenton was a whiz-kid the project could do well without.

As Pippa watched Fenton stacking the luggage she was smiling at the way Mike had written it down. He should have been a diplomat not an archaeologist. Suddenly, she felt a tiny throb of excitement at the prospect of seeing Mike again. He hadn't written to her often on this trip. Mike didn't show his feelings that much, but Pippa had always known they were on the same wavelength.

The previous year, a lot of Pippa's working days and lonely nights had been centred on Mike Nash. She remembered especially the afternoon they had visited the British Museum. Mike hadn't talked much. He seemed lost in his own thoughts as they had wandered, hand in hand, through the enormous galleries, looking at the statues and artefacts.

Naturally enough, their wanderings led them to the Egyptology department where they had sauntered from glass case to glass case looking at the wrapped bodies of the mummies and all the wonderful things to be found in dead kings' tombs.

Their reflections had stared back at them dimly and Pippa remembered what she'd said. "Is something the matter, Mike?"

"No, not really," he answered, his pale face almost white in the gloom of the gallery. "I was just thinking about leaving you." Her heart had plummeted, then risen again. He was going to miss her when he went off to Cairo to join her father.

"Never mind, Mike. I'll be out to see you." But, inside, she knew how busy she was and how long it was going to be before they were together properly again.

Later, they had lain in silence after making love back at Pippa's flat. Pippa ran a tender hand over Mike's body and he quivered at her touch. "We *will* be together again, Mike," she said.

"I hope so, darling." Then he'd brushed her lips with his own cool ones and got up to dress. Sometimes, Pippa had wished he was more passionate but he was, after all, a scientist. And Pippa knew what that meant very well. Sacrifice after sacrifice - and very little home life.

One day, perhaps, a man in her life, like her father or Mike, might ask her to go out to Egypt with him. But she knew better. Both Mike and Dad were married to their work.

Then her father had spirited him away to the Cairo site. Mike had joined the team after several years in South America and Pippa thought she had got to know him very well.

He had written her some letters when he was over in Colombia first, but they'd thinned out after a while. Pippa was used to that. She'd enjoyed hearing about all the goings-on in that volatile country and she made the best of it by answering promptly.

It had been the same in Egypt. Mike's letters had become fewer which meant surely that her father was keeping her boy friend far too busy...

"Penny for them," Rik Fenton said as he opened the driver's door and got into his seat.

"Oh, they were worth far more than that," Pippa replied. He glanced at her and there was mischief in his eyes.

"There won't be much time for dreaming out there," he added as he swung the car on to the road into crazy traffic. "The desert brings its own illusions."

"I suppose you do a lot of dreaming?" Pippa asked sarcastically.

"Only when I have something worthwhile to imagine," he countered, taking his eyes off the road for a moment to stare at her. They were attractive eyes but they had dark rings under them. Fenton must have been working very hard too.

Pippa ignored the remark and looked out of the window, concentrating on the glittering city they were skirting.

"Have you been to Cairo before?" he asked.

"Once when I was very small. But I don't remember much."

"Good. Shall I give you the tourist *spiel* then?"

"If you like." Of course, he'd be sure to know everything about everything. He had that air of arrogance about him.

"Most of the business life of the city is on the east bank of the Nile. We're going west towards Giza. But, if you get the chance, you should go and see the old city, which is east of the modern business centre. It's amazing."

"I'd like to," Pippa replied as they cruised on from the airport through the Heliopolis district.

"Of course, there's an enormous amount of poverty," he said. "Thousands of the poorest people live in a depressed area they call *The City of the Dead*."

"Sounds horrible," Pippa grimaced.

"I promise you it is. But it's the only place they can find to live. An area of cemeteries. They sleep in crypts and mausoleums, you know."

"Ugh," said Pippa, trying to decide if he was lecturing her. "But you should be used to those."

"I am, but I'm an archaeologist. I do my job for historical reasons. I think modern politicians should take care of such problems." Rik Fenton uttered the statement so forcefully that Pippa wasn't sure whether to carry on the conversation or not. Still, it was good someone cared.

10

Neither spoke after that for a while. Then Rik Fenton began pointing out major tourist sites while Pippa studied his handsome profile. He was a very interesting man but she'd have preferred it if he'd given her time to say something. Perhaps he was nervous of women though? But she doubted it. However, he knew a lot about Egypt.

It wasn't until they were on the western bank of the Nile and making for the desert that Pippa asked, "How is the work on the site going?"

"Slowly. Mike Nash is in a bit of a hurry though. He likes to put on the pressure."

"I should think that's fairly praise-worthy," Pippa said, sensing the criticism in Fenton's voice.

"You think so?" He was manoeuvering the vehicle skilfully.

"Why shouldn't I?"

"Because, Miss Adams, archaeology is a very precise science. If you go too fast, you can miss something important."

"I know that," she said indignantly, thinking that Mike had been right about this man. He was too self-assured, and confident. "I have spent quite a bit of time out on sites myself."

"Then you'll know what I mean," Rik replied shortly.

* * *

By the time she saw the cluster of huts and tents coming out of a shimmering heat haze, Pippa was realising there was going to be some tension between her and the abrupt, young man whose eyes pierced the sand in front of him like some sharp-eyed hawk. It was then a tall, gangling figure hurried out of his tent.

11

"Pippa!" He was coming towards the car. Her father looked greyer than she'd ever seen him. His hair and beard were quite white. "I'm sorry I didn't come but Mike and I have been extremely rushed," he began.

"Yes, Rik told me. That's all right, Dad."

She was out of the car and into his arms in seconds. As her father embraced her, her eyes were searching for Mike, but he didn't appear. Then Professor Adams let his daughter go and looked at her with some emotion.

"This job is a devil," he said. "It seems like years since I saw you. You're thinner."

"Not quite that long, Dad. Months actually," she teased, looking him over in turn. "And *archaeology* is the devil himself. You don't look as though Egypt's doing you much good."

"It's the heat. I should be used to it but, at the moment, it's very uncomfortable. However, it's the work which is important, not me."

Pippa sighed. She'd heard it all before. She looked over to where she could see Rik Fenton unloading some of her luggage, but where on earth was Mike?

"He's over there, Pippa," Rik called as he lifted two of her heaviest cases out quite easily. Somehow the remark sounded flippant. How had he guessed she wanted to see Mike?

"Oh, I'm sorry, my dear, Mike's in his tent. He's going over a few things I left him; some of the lists of the most interesting finds," her father said apologetically. "You want to see him, of course. Come on, I'll take you."

As they walked over, the native workers were watching her every movement in silence but, all the time, Pippa was wondering why Mike hadn't come out to meet her. She followed her father over to a large tent with an awning. Professor Fenton peered through the flap. "She's here, Mike."

"Excellent!" a voice said from inside. Next moment, her father was ushering her through. Mike was seated at a small table, heaped with paperwork. He started to his feet as she crossed over to him.

"Pippa! How are you, darling?" It had only been six months but there was an awkwardness in his manner that stopped her kissing him. Did he expect her to? She couldn't tell from his face.

"I'm fine," she said. Then, he was coming round the table and holding out his arms. She walked into them.

"I'll leave you two together then," said her father tactfully. "See you soon, darling."

He withdrew. Pippa looked up into Mike's eyes. He kissed her on the forehead. He looked much older, too. His fair hair was thinning and his skin was tight and drawn. The climate played havoc with Europeans.

"I'm sorry, love. I should have come to meet you myself but I was . . ."

"Busy?" She smiled.

"Was Fenton late?" Mike was frowning.

"No. The plane was," Rik said, pushing through the flap with the suitcases.

Pippa thought how tactless it was for him to walk in just like that - especially when she and Mike wanted some quiet moments together.

"Do you want your case in here?"

"Drop them, Rik. I'll take them to Pippa's tent." Mike's tone was cold.

"Suits me." Rik grinned, but Pippa could see the smile didn't reach his eyes. "I'm not particularly good at portering anyway." He walked out just as abruptly.

Pippa watched him go then turned to Mike. "He says what he means, doesn't he?"

"Unfortunately." She had never seen Mike look so grim. His lips were set in a pale line, sharp against his tan. "Fenton is a law unto himself." Mike looked down at Pippa. "Don't let's waste time talking about him, Pippa. Tell me what you've been doing with yourself."

"Oh, the usual. Overflowing with patients, I'm afraid."

"But that's good, isn't it?"

"Yes. I love my job, as you know but, sometimes, I feel trapped. As if the whole of the world is breaking down - and I'm having to treat the lot of them." She sat on a canvas stool while Mike went over and sat some distance from her on his narrow bed.

At first, she felt she would go and sit close to him but there was something in his manner which stopped her. Was it possible he didn't care any more? After all, his letters had petered out.

"We all feel like that sometimes, I think," he said, staring down at the ground sheet.

"You're all right, aren't you, Mike? Out here? The wild open spaces. All that sand," she joked. "At least, it's not like claustrophobic old London and the awful grind of commuting every day."

"Sounds good to me," was the surprising reply.

"You mean you're so fed up you want to go *home*. What would Dad say about you going back to London?"

"London's not home for me, Pippa," replied Mike.

"Why not? You were born in Acton."

"I'd rather forget that," he retorted. "Although I'm fed up, I don't want to return to England. I'd like to go back to South America."

"Colombia?" She hoped the disappointment wouldn't

show in her voice. She could never imagine living there. It would be nice for a holiday, but not for ever.

"That's right," he said. "Fat chance there is of that though with all this work. I don't think we'll ever crack this bloody dig." He brushed several flies from round his head. "Now - can't we talk about something different?"

"If you like," replied Pippa. "What?" She was running out of ideas already.

They went on to the dig. Questions about what had been found and when. Lists. It was quite hard work talking to Mike. She'd never thought so before. She put it down to the long flight. Coupled with the heat, all she wanted now was food and bed. If the latter had included Mike, it would have been wonderful but, somehow, by the look on his face and his whole attitude, that seemed the remotest possibility indeed.

* * *

CHAPTER 2

They didn't talk for much longer as Professor Adams sent a boy to tell them dinner was ready. Mike let Pippa walk out in front of the tent before he followed. He was settling his Panama over his brow when he came stooping out in the evening sunlight. Pippa waited, her eyes taking in everything around her. In the distance she could see Rik Fenton talking to a group of native workers.

"You wouldn't think under there was so precious," she said. To the eye of a novice all it looked like were great mounds of sand. "Have you found heaps of interesting things?"

"Yes, but - dinner won't wait. Come on, you must be famished."

It had been the same the whole of their conversation. Once, Mike had been eager to talk about everything; now, he seemed to have lost all his enthusiasm. Every question she had asked about the new tomb they were excavating had been pushed aside skilfully and the subject changed. *But that doesn't matter*, Pippa thought, looking into his face, *at least we're together again.*

London seemed millions of miles away as they walked across the sands towards the small tent that served as cookhouse for the site.

A wiry, little Arab handed her the soup. He had the litheness of a cat and his face was lean and wrinkled. He didn't smile.

"Meet Ahmed." Her father laughed. "He can turn his hand to anything. I really don't know what on earth we would do without him."

The man bowed at the compliment, fixing Pippa with expressionless dark eyes. For a moment, she thought there was something hostile in his look but dismissed the thought as nonsensical.

Don't be silly, Pippa, she told herself, *you just can't relax, can you? Always analysing everyone and everything.* The clinic where she worked as a psychologist was in the smartest part of London and Pippa was tired of making big decisions about other people's personal lives instead of her own.

As she sipped her soup and looked across the golden-brown landscape, she knew she wanted to forget it all and only think about her future with Mike Nash.

"Did you know that the Nile is just over there?" Rik Fenton asked, breaking into her private thoughts once more. She looked into his challenging eyes.

"Is it? It doesn't look like it."

"Yes," her father added, "the tombs here stand on the edge of the desert. Even in ancient times the Egyptians used every available inch near to the river to plant their crops. The Nile was their only lifeline."

Pippa couldn't imagine that there could be anything green nearby. The land seemed incredibly barren as far as one could see.

They sat in their camp chairs, trying to relax, their bodies strung up in the tormenting heat. Professor Adams mopped his forehead every minute while Pippa thought longingly of the great water over the desert edge.

"Is it always as hot as this?" she said. "I'd almost forgotten."

"Yes," Rik Fenton answered shortly.

"Would you like me to take you back to your tent?" Mike asked.

"It's better for Pippa out here," Rik Fenton said slowly, then he turned to her. "It's murder in the tents in the heat of the evening."

There was silence.

Then she said, "Yes, I would prefer it out here, thank you, Mike. I suppose it's fresher."

Mike didn't say a thing, only looked at Rik. Suddenly, Pippa was realising that another tension was adding to the heat of the atmosphere.

"It's hotter than Morocco," she said to her father, deliberately trying to turn the conversation. "Do you remember that terrible summer, Dad?"

"How could I possibly forget?" he said quietly, closing his eyes. They sat in silence. Pippa was angry with herself for being so insensitive. Morocco had seemed a very long time ago. It had also been the last time she'd seen her mother. . .

Professor Adams had been supervising a dig in a very bleak part of the North African desert. Pippa remembered the remoteness of the site. It was much more isolated than the one in Cairo.

She had been eleven years old at the time and had just started in the senior part of her English convent boarding school the September before. However, that warm European autumn had seemed far away compared with the blazing heat of Africa.

She didn't want to think of school because it meant leaving Mummy. She was fairly used to her father going away but, this time, her mother was going to stay on site with him. So Pippa had been determined to make the most of her extended holiday in Morocco.

Why hadn't she noticed that her mother was very thin and coughed a great deal? Although Pippa used to play games in the sand and show her mother the stones she'd collected, Mummy didn't take a great deal of notice.

Why hadn't it sunk in when she heard her mother and father quarrelling about going back to England with Pippa? Her father kept saying, "Your place is with the child, Sheila. Please go home. It isn't that long to be apart really. I'll be back. And you know you're unwell."

She'd never heard her mother answer because Pippa had run off. She'd always felt those rows were her fault; that in some way she'd caused the widening breach between her parents.

If it hadn't been for her, then her mother could have stayed all the time in Morocco and her father wouldn't have had to worry. Quite often, on that holiday, she would sit outside Dad's tent and then he'd appear and, stooping, pick her up and piggy back her to some heap of dusty artefacts that had been dug up from the rock-hard earth.

After, he'd set her down and show her the finds, explaining their origins as he went over each carefully. She had learned to sift and wash, to arrange and classify. No wonder she was one of the best in history lessons at school. Yes, Pippa had cut her teeth on antiques literally. She remembered one particular time when she'd been sitting on her father's knee. He'd been unusually quiet after a recent row and she'd looked up into his tanned face and those deep, intelligent eyes.

He'd gazed back and said, "You get more like your mother every day, Pippa."

"I don't, I don't," she'd retorted, wanting to be her own person even at eleven. Inside, she wanted to say, "That's good, isn't it, Daddy? You love Mummy, don't you?" But she couldn't.

And that's why, when she grew up, she'd found a job as a psychologist, trying to help people to be able to talk and rationalise their fears. That summer had been the last her father had spent with his wife and Pippa. Her mother had died on the site the following year.

She'd had a sudden fever and it had turned to pneumonia too quickly for even a helicopter to bring out a doctor. Later, Pippa had learned illness had always been a real fear for her father. Taking his wife and child some place where there wasn't decent and immediate medical attention had worried him a great deal. But her mother had been stubborn. Pippa concluded it was because Mummy loved him so much - and probably better than her.

It was just before the Easter vacation when Mother Superior had brought the news. Pippa was about to go off to stay with an aunt in London for the spring break.

As Pippa finished the soup, she remembered how she'd been sitting in the refectory with her friends, chattering happily about the coming holiday.

"Look out. Here's Reverend Mother."

They were all wondering what they'd done when Pippa was singled out.

Sister's kind face looked extremely worried under the snowy wimple. "Pippa. Hello, dear. I'd like to have a word."

"Yes, Reverend Mother?" Pippa was going over everything she'd done wrong in the week before.

"In my office, please." Her friends looked scared as Pippa followed the nun. It was the first time Pippa had ever been in there. There were some details she still remembered clearly. The large crucifix on the wall and a picture of the Pope.

Reverend Mother seated herself opposite Pippa, who was trembling. "I'm afraid I've some bad news, Pippa, dear. Sit down, child," she had said. "Your mother has died. In Morocco. Shall we say a little prayer for her?" Pippa didn't hear a word.

All she could think of was that she wouldn't see her mother any more. Here today and gone the next. The headmistress didn't elaborate on the tragedy. It had been pneumonia, she said.

Pippa never even went to her mother's funeral over there because a person had to be buried so quickly in hot countries like that. She had just been left to grieve all by herself until her father came home. . .

It had been an enormous blow to the professor. He had lost both a helpmate and a companion. He had never been the same since his wife died - he just worked himself like a horse trying to forget.

And twenty-four year old Pippa had never had the opportunity to get close to him really since. To speak about her mother's death. She'd always believed he'd loved her mother better than her.

Inside, there was a small part of her that was sure he spent such a lot of time away because Pippa reminded him too much of what he'd lost. It was a silly notion, but she couldn't get over the feeling and the remembrance of those rows. If only she could. She wanted to desperately.

Pippa put out her hand and touched her father on the arm. "It's great we're together again, Dad," she said and closed his rough, wrinkled hand over hers.

Rik Fenton smiled at them and stretched his long frame as he got out of the small chair. He was yawning again. "Well, Pippa, what are you going to do all the time you're visiting?"

"I was hoping to get a good look at Egypt."

"Well, you can't do it on your own. Can she, Mike?"

Pippa could hear the challenge in the man's voice. She waited to hear Mike agree with him; to tell him that he would be by her side.

Instead he said, "I suppose not but, unfortunately I'm busy at the moment." He turned to Pippa. "You see, we've just started transporting items from the bottom level."

"You don't have to make excuses, Mike," Pippa said brightly. "I do understand, you know."

Professor Adams looked at Rik, then at Pippa. "I'm extremely tied-up as well," he said. There was an edge to his voice. "Mike and I have to catalogue the stuff for government purposes and . . ."

"And you don't have to make excuses either, Dad," she said, squeezing his arm affectionately and trying to conceal the flat disappointment in her tone.

"We could get Ahmed to take you," Mike said. His voice echoed eerily as the night winds sprang up and tossed it against the rocks behind.

"No," Rik Fenton said, "I'll do the taking, as I seem to be at a loose end for the next few days." He turned to Professor Adams. "That's if you don't mind, sir."

He ignored Mike. Pippa could see then just what kind of friction there was between the two young men.

"No," she said suddenly, "I'll stay around here, if you don't mind, Dad, until Mike can find the time to take me."

There was silence. And then her father stood up slowly

and looked across in the direction of the tomb, staring at the scaffolding that surrounded it.

"Pippa, I would rather that Mike and I got on as arranged. Rik's branch of the work is over for the moment. Of course, we could do with him - but I can spare him more easily than Mike."

Pippa realised that her father was saying Mike couldn't go. She was amazed. He was always easy-going, never dogmatic.

"OK, Dad, if that's what you want."

"Thank you, Pippa." Professor Adams stuck his hands in his pockets and looked at the sunset.

"What *do* you want, John?" The woman's voice came from behind them.

"Mia, my dear," Professor Adams said. "Come and meet my daughter."

Pippa looked up into dark eyes. The woman was aged about thirty-five, with strong features that were handsome rather than pretty. She had a confident air about her and was dressed in bush jacket and trousers.

"Mia," Rik said and kissed her on both cheeks. "Allow me to introduce Dr. Mia Gabal, our trusted colleague and very good friend."

"Hello, Pippa," she said. Pippa could see Rik was still holding her hand.

"Hello. Are you working on the site?"

"She certainly is," Rik said. "And we couldn't do without her." Mia and Rik exchanged glances.

"Are you an archaeologist, Doctor?" Pippa asked.

"Yes - but don't let's talk about work," Mia Gabal sat down. "I've heard so much about you, Pippa. I've been looking forward to meeting you."

"Have you?" Pippa asked. "From whom?"

"Why, John has told me everything - and Mike, of course."

"Of course," Rik Fenton said.

Mike stood up, frowning. "Come on, Pippa," he said. "Let's take the jeep and I'll show you the Nile."

"Hey, Mike, take Mia with you. She'll be able to give Pippa all the local colour," Rik Fenton said, catching at his arm.

"I'd be absolutely delighted," Mia Gabal said jumping up. "And why don't you come, too, John?"

"No, really," Professor Adams said, "I have to stay and look over the notes."

"Right," Rik said, "we'll look them over together, sir. And, Pippa, let's make it the Pyramids tomorrow, eh?"

"If you like," Pippa said stiffly.

It seemed she and Mike were not going to get any time alone together on this site, especially now they had Mia Gabal in tow. The three of them walked towards the jeep, Pippa and Mia on each side with Mike in the middle.

* * *

CHAPTER 3

Pippa was glad that Mia Gabal had gone with them after all. She certainly knew everything of interest. She started as soon as they swung out of the camp site, past the native workmen huddled in their robes ready for sleep.

"Are you Egyptian, Mia?" Pippa asked, wishing she was the one to be sitting by Mike.

"Through and through, as you English say. This is my home." Mia swept her arm around indicating the desert.

Mike didn't speak, only drove on towards the horizon, over the dunes.

Pippa gasped at the wonderful view. Suddenly, instead of brown, there was deep, blue sapphire becoming dark purple in the distance. The great river was so broad it seemed to have no opposite bank. Except for a splash of dark green in the distance, Pippa could only see the water. Above, sugar-pink clouds drifted in the last rays of the sun.

"It's all so clear," Pippa gasped.

"Here," Mia Gabal said, handing her a sweater. "Put this on. The night chills come down fast."

The three of them watched the white sails of native feluccas drifting lazily across the blue expanse. At the very edge of the Nile, dark figures were silhouetted against the sky, driving their cattle.

"Without the Nile we would not survive," Mia said softly.

Pippa wished she could sit there for ever watching the river. There was only one thing that worried her. Mike was sitting like a stone seeming not to be taking notice of anything that was said.

"Isn't it a fantastic view, Mike?" she said, trying to bring him into the conversation. He was still looking in front of him with unseeing eyes.

"I suppose so." He shrugged as he answered. "But as far as I'm concerned, it's nothing compared to South America." The remark seemed like a direct insult to the woman seated between them.

"Oh, come on, Mike," Pippa said, ashamed for herself and him, "you don't really mean that, do you?"

"Do not apologise for Mr. Nash," the archaeologist said. "He and I understand each other very well." With that, she put out her hand and switched on the ignition and headlights.

As the jeep lurched over the uneven terrain, Pippa sat miserably silent. It seemed that all she had hoped for on this holiday was disappearing slowly. There was friction everywhere - just as there was in London. Evidently relationships on the camp site were very poor indeed.

She glanced at Mike as he drove, back straight; at Mia Gabal, who jolted up and down with the jeep, putting up her hand occasionally to throw back her mane of long black hair. *What has happened to you, Mike?* Pippa thought. *You weren't like this in London. Then you were alive - now you seem to be dead inside.* Pippa remembered the warmth they had shared - and the laughter. What had Egypt done to Mike Nash and her father?

Suddenly, she was thinking of Rik Fenton. However

brash he was, he seemed alive. There was something about the man which attracted her to him in spite of his rudeness. Perhaps it was his frankness Pippa liked. She detested deception of any kind; it was too much to bear after dealing with it from her patients day in day out.

It came to her then that Mike had never really been open with her. Perhaps this was what he was really like though, and she'd been too blind to see it. Pippa broke off the thought suddenly, feeling guilty at such disloyalty. Mike was looking at her.

"Five minutes, Pippa, then you can get some rest," he said, breaking into her thoughts.

"I'm not particularly tired. I don't suppose jet-lag has set in yet," she said.

"It would be advisable for you to get an early night, Pippa," Mia Gabal said. "If I know Rik Fenton, you have a full day ahead."

"And you do know him, don't you, Mia?" Mike grunted.

The bitterness in his tones stunned Pippa. There was something going on in this project; everyone was pulling different ways. But why? She shook her head sadly, all of a sudden wondering if coming to Egypt had been such a good idea after all.

* * *

"Good-night then, Pippa, sleep well," Mike said. On the plane to Cairo she had imagined kissing him; now would have been just the time, but he was not going to, and she was not sure she wanted him to. He just leaned forward and pulled back the tent flap.

"Mike," she said, "what's the matter?"

"Nothing," he answered abruptly. "Why?"

"You seem . . . different."

"How?" But she knew he understood.

"In London . . ." she began.

"This is Egypt." He stated the fact baldly.

"Does it make a difference?"

"I think you've had a very tiring day. Why don't we talk about it tomorrow?"

"All right, Mike," she replied. "We'll talk tomorrow."

Pippa watched him walk away between the tents; saw him talk to Ahmed, the dark Arab; she was still staring as they walked out of her line of vision.

She lay on her narrow camp bed, thinking of Mike and her father. When they had come back, her father had been poring over ledgers, a weary expression on his face. Filling his life with work was doing him a lot of harm.

As for Mike - Pippa sighed and stared up at the canvas from under her mosquito net. She was trying to analyse her feelings in a professional way. She had looked forward so long to seeing him; kept the old vision of him in her heart for six months. But this was a different man she was seeing.

Why, Mike, why? Pippa thought. *Why did I think we were in love?* She kept on staring until the gas lantern hurt her eyes, the same questions going round and round inside her head

* * *

She woke early, opening the tent flap to the dawn. She had no idea when they were going to start off but, in the distance, she could see Rik preparing for the day's work. He seemed such a vibrant, athletic figure in this valley of the dead. Behind him, the excavations loomed eerily, and the rising sun caught him in its light, bathing his strong frame, stripped to the waist, in a warm rose-pink, almost making a statue out of him.

Inexplicably, her spirits lifted. She was suddenly glad that it was Rik who was taking her to see the Pharaohs' tombs. She had always wanted to see the Pyramids properly ever since she had been a little girl looking at the coloured plates in her father's books.

As she mulled over why Mike had fallen out of love with her, she suddenly realised she was wondering what it would be like to fall in love with Rik Fenton.

Suddenly, he turned. Next moment, he was striding over towards her tent. Pippa unzipped the flap but immediately realised her baby-doll pyjamas were quite inadequate for entertaining.

"Why aren't you asleep?" he asked. Every word he uttered was a challenge.

"I often wake up at dawn," she replied. "There isn't a law against it." Her eyes flashed at his arrogance.

"And no doubt you're always as prickly."

"Prickly? *I am not*." She was bristling with the insult. "In fact, I'm well-known for my good temper."

"All the time?" His amused eyes strafed her face. She flushed, then regained her composure. Pushing her hair out of her eyes, she realised that Rik Fenton was glancing at her over-exposed cleavage.

"You're very rude, Mr. Fenton."

"Yes, I call a spade a spade. It goes with the job."

"Being too blunt isn't always a good thing," she retorted.

"And you'd know, of course."

"It's *my* job." Next moment, Rik put out his hand and

touched her hair. "What are you doing?" She jumped, ready to jerk away ever further.

"Stand still," he commanded. "There's a spider in your hair."

"A spider?" She froze.

"Got it." She opened her eyes into his. "It was a very small one." The amused look on his face was insufferable.

"I don't believe there was one. How could you?"

"I assume from your face you're not keen on spiders. And, I assure you, there *was* one."

They were so close she could feel the warmth of his breath. However much she tried, Pippa couldn't keep thrilling to his nearness.

"Well, thank you," she murmured. Next moment, she felt his strong fingers close on her forearm.

"I'd get dressed if I were you," he said. "Otherwise the moskies will have you next." He smiled. "But . . . you look great. In spite of your temper." Pippa could hardly believe his arrogance. How dare he compliment her with *that look* in his eyes. Suddenly, he bent and kissed her on the cheek.

She jerked back her head in annoyance. "Are you usually as forward as this, Rik Fenton?"

"Oh, much worse. I'm afraid it's another of my failings, complimenting beautiful women." His eyes were searching her face.

She flushed and not only from the heat. "I can believe that. Now, please go away. I'm going back to bed."

His impudent grin broadened. "I wish I was," he said. "But I've got work to do. I'll see you later."

Next moment, he was striding away into the dawn, making for the excavations where several workers were already emerging from their tents. Pippa zipped up the tent flap and, suddenly, her cheeks flamed as she imagined

30

what it would be like *going back to bed* with the enigmatic Rik Fenton. She had a very strange dream after the encounter. . .

She was floating down the Nile on a felucca. She was dressed like Cleopatra. A bare-breasted servant, who looked like Mia Gabal, was fanning her with ostrich feathers. Seated beside Pippa was the Pharoah - and he had a face like Rik's. Just as Pippa turned to speak loving words to him, he ignored her. Next moment he was leaning over to kiss Mia Gabal full on the mouth. . .

Pippa woke up suddenly, feeling angry and disappointed. Half-asleep, she pummelled her pillow in disgust. It was then she realised where she was. In her tent in Egypt on holiday. And it had only been a dream. Whatever was the matter with her?

* * *

Rik was determined to tell Pippa everything about where they were going, and she had to admit to herself, although he was arrogant, he was a fascinating guy. She really wanted to know the history and he was ready to tell her. Some things you just couldn't learn from books.

"Egyptian pyramids date from about 2700BC to about 1000BC," he said as they loomed up in the distance. "The Great Pyramid is one of the old Seven Wonders of the World. It's the tomb of the Pharoah Khufu. 481 feet high."

"And that's exact?" asked Pippa. He glanced at her sharply and she was immediately sorry. "Oh, I don't mean to sound rude; it's just you're blinding me with science. . . Dates and such."

"I thought you wanted the details." He grinned, returning to his driving. He wasn't annoyed after all. In fact, he was very easy to get on with. Pippa knew one of her main strengths was listening. But in her job, it was she who had to supply the answers. Now she was on the receiving end.

However, Rik was using historical knowledge for his solutions. She had to flounder about looking for them. That was the difference between him and her. Rik Fenton appeared to have no grey areas in his life.

She stole several glances at him as he drove the jeep. She didn't like to stare too much as Ahmed was sitting behind her and would notice. She wished they hadn't had to bring him but, according to Rik, there was a good reason.

Anyway, the man seemed to be asleep just then, so Pippa continued her appraisal. Suddenly, her dream was fresh in her mind. *The Pharoah had probably looked just like Rik Fenton; that straight nose, aquiline features, piercing eyes.*

Suddenly, he took his eyes off the road and caught hers.

"Shall I continue? Or have you had enough?"

"No, go on, please."

"Well, we're going to Saqquara as well. To see the step pyramid. It was built about 2700 BC. . ." Rik told her although the Middle Kingdom was his main field, he was researching other Dynasties besides the Eleventh.

The conversation was so interesting that they arrived at the taxis, which took them to the foot of the pyramids, in what seemed a very short time. And then their exhausting day had really begun.

Soon Pippa found herself scrambling up a pyramid. These days it was forbidden to climb them, but the authorities had made an exception as Professor Adams was a well-known figure in government circles. So the professor's daughter, Rik and the servant, Ahmed had obtained permission. And, occasionally, she wished they hadn't.

They were almost at the top of the pyramid, but Pippa was so breathless she couldn't tell how far they had to go. She looked up into the sky towards Rik Fenton.

"Can you make it?" he shouted, stretching down a strong hand.

"Of course I can," she gasped at last, feeling the stone with her feet. "It wasn't that bad." She looked at Rik's quizzical eyebrows raised triumphantly and felt extremely irritated.

"You look great," he said, surprising her.

Pippa brushed back her long hair, wet with perspiration. She felt breathless and hot. His manner was so cool, but she could see the tell-tale sweat stains across the front of his khaki shirt.

"She's done well, hasn't she, Ahmed?" The barefoot guide grinned, but the smile didn't reach all the way across his monkey-like face. "You can do it in how long?" he asked the Egyptian.

"When alone, I climb the pyramid in ten minutes."

Pippa gasped, her face showing disbelief as Ahmed continued, "Sadly I do not hold the record, sir. There is one man who can do it in seven," he added proudly.

"And it took us an hour," Rik said.

Pippa thought he was criticising her. She was about to utter a sarcastic remark when she swayed dizzily.

"Hey, hold on," he said. "You'd better sit down."

She did so very quickly because her legs were trembling and she needed Rik's arm to hold on to. She was angry with herself for feeling so exhausted.

"Any better now?" He was exasperating; amazingly fit

33

and seemingly indestructible in that blazing Egyptian morning.

"Yes," she replied, looking round her at the view from the top. It was awesome. Across and beyond the desert, the dark triangle of another pyramid was silhouetted in the sun.

"The Monument of Cephren," Rik said, following her gaze, "a son of Cheops."

"Oh," she said, wishing she had known it.

"Impressive, isn't it?"

So he felt the same. He wasn't patronising her now - and he should have known. He was already an eminent archaeologist at just thirty-two. She was sure both he and the world knew that. "Imagine, Pippa, four thousand years. Four and a half to be exact. Look at the stones you're sitting on."

"Of course we have to be exact," she muttered sarcastically, but she did look down at the massive blocks. Age-old vandals had carved their names all over them with signs and symbols.

"It's very interesting, but all I can think of now is we have to go down again."

He laughed, and Ahmed turned and looked at them with expressionless eyes.

"Well, we can't stay up here. What would your father say?"

He had certainly said something when he'd heard Pippa wanted to climb a pyramid. She could still hear the words when they started out in the morning.

"Pippa, you'll exhaust yourself - and it's very dangerous. One slip and that'll be it."

"I'll be OK," she had protested.

"You'd better be. But I trust Fenton. He'll look after you."

"I can look after myself, Dad."

She knew she was being treated like a child. She couldn't tell her father that she wasn't that keen on his brilliant *protégé*. It was Rik Fenton's arrogance that irritated her most of all. He made her feel ten instead of twenty-four. But then she remembered her dream again. Was there anything between him and Mia Gabal?

She looked across to where Ahmed was still sitting on the edge of the stones, head bent, recouping his strength. Why couldn't Rik Fenton look a bit like that instead of standing staring out across the desert as if he owned it?

She couldn't explain even to herself why she felt that about the man. She could almost imagine that if he stretched out those muscular arms and took off, he would swoop across the valley like an eagle. Rik would always fall on his feet. He'd certainly done so with her father.

Professor Adams had marked him out from the beginning. Pippa remembered the first time he'd mentioned Rik in a letter. . .

". . . Oh, and I have a brilliant new postgraduate student. . ." It was the first time too that she'd ever heard her father use the word *brilliant*. ". . . he's a specialist in the Middle Kingdom and, as I'm expecting to work on an excavation in this period in a year or so, I couldn't do better than to take him along when the thesis is finished."

So after supervising Rik's brilliant research, Professor Fenton had rushed off to Cairo with him and they'd been there ever since, excavating a university project. It was later that he had Mike Nash join him, who'd also been one of his students and, for some reason, had been released early from a South American government project.

Pippa wondered if her father sometimes regretted she hadn't chosen to become an archaeologist like him. But,

35

given what had happened to her mother, she supposed he was content to see her working in London as a psychologist and just making trips to him occasionally in all those foreign places.

Of course, she would have liked more personal contact but, in archaeology, it was often impossible. She was sure her father could have gone back to a desk job at the university but he'd always resisted that. He said there was too much administration these days and it wasn't his strong point. He evidently left Rik and Mia Gabal the organisation of the dig. So she might as well make the most of the chances she had. It was ages since he'd worked in Egypt. Therefore, she intended to have a damn good holiday in a place she'd always wanted to go since she'd read one of her father's books on the Valley of the Kings.

And, of course, being with Mike was a bonus too. . . Then she realised Rik was staring down at her. Suddenly Pippa was in the defensive again.

"Am I keeping you waiting? Are you ready to go now?"

"If *you* are. And don't worry about it." He peered down the dizzy drop. "You'll be all right with me."

"I'd hate to slow you down." She couldn't help her tone.

"You won't. It's been a welcome change taking you."

"How very nice of you to say so." Pippa bent and examined her bootlaces.

"Why don't you take them off? Ahmed climbs in bare feet."

"You don't expect me to, I hope."

"No," he said shortly. "And we don't have to go down yet - and I meant that you could take off your boots and give your feet a breather."

36

He turned back to the view again as Pippa struggled with the laces. The climb had been very exhausting and her fingers were trembling, making the task almost impossible.

Suddenly, Rik Fenton was squatting beside her. "Here, let me help you," he offered.

"I can manage."

"I don't think so," he said and, with a swift movement, he had the laces untied and was pulling off her boots.

"Oh, that's better," she gasped in relief, but she could see several blisters coming up on her toes.

"We'll have to see to those," Rik Fenton said, "otherwise you won't be sight-seeing tomorrow." He took out a little phial from his small rucksack and rubbed the liquid on the bubbles. She relaxed under the gentle pressure.

"That's better," he said, almost to himself. The intimate moment made Pippa feel a little ashamed of herself. Had she been a bit hard on him?

"Wake up, Ahmed," he said, jumping and shaking the man by the shoulder. "I wouldn't like to go to sleep on the edge of a pyramid." He laughed. "Would you?"

The question was directed at Pippa and she smiled then, catching the joke. The sun was burning her toes above and the stone was hot beneath her feet.

"You'll have to put them on again," he warned, indicating the boots.

"I know that," she snapped and their sunny moment was gone.

With Ahmed leading, they began the descent. It was much worse going down. This time she wasn't sure she'd make it. Although she had a head for heights, several times she thought she would fall, but

Rik was always there steadying her progress. By the time an hour had passed she knew her father's words had been very true. She was certainly safe with Rik Fenton.

"How much longer?" she asked.

"I'm afraid it's going to take more than an hour this way." He looked up into her eyes.

"I shall have to rest."

"Ahmed," he called. "Look at that fellow. He's leaping about like a goat."

Pippa couldn't understand how the man could do it. She just sat down wearily exactly where she was. Rik was standing beside her.

"Over there," he said, pointing, "that's Cairo. We can't see the West, that's Africa. I expect you'd like to see inside the pyramid now."

"Not just now," she said. Sometimes he was insufferable.

"Oh, come on. You must see inside."

He didn't seem to have noticed her tone. "I'm sure your dad won't mind."

"Do you always do what he says?" Pippa was sorry after the sentence slipped out.

He was looking at her as if she was a little child. "He's the boss. I owe my job to him. What he says goes. And I'm very grateful to him."

"Do you know, Rik Fenton, you're too good to be true," she retorted.

He looked down at her. "So that's what you think, is it?"

"Yes."

"Remind me to show you otherwise - sometime."

She was annoyed with herself for behaving so childishly.

38

It was just that Rik Fenton kept getting under her skin. . .

Ten minutes later, they were disappearing inside the pyramid with Pippa wondering what exactly he had meant by saying, "Remind me to show you sometime."

Once they had entered the pyramid, Pippa was glad that Rik had been able to spare the time to bring her here after all. She knew that accompanying Rik Fenton to the tomb of a great Pharaoh, was a million times more exciting than being escorted by the barefoot Ahmed - or Mike.

"You're not tired already?" Rik asked. "There's acres to cover yet."

"I'm only stopping to catch my breath," Pippa said.

"Why don't you admit it?" he said smiling. "You feel worn out and could do with a drink."

She wondered if he was teasing her on purpose. He bent uncomfortably to draw the flask round his back. "Here you are."

"Thanks," she said, putting the flask to her lips. The water tasted brackish and unpleasant. "The only good thing about that is it's wet." She handed it back.

"You'd be glad of it if you were in the desert," he commented, putting his lips to the neck.

"We are," she said.

"Outside, I mean."

"I know. I was just being awkward."

"So you admit it, Miss Adams." His eyes smiled and mocked at the same time.

"Don't patronise me, Mr. Fenton," she retorted.

"You know," Rik said, looking her in the eyes, "I'm beginning to wish I hadn't brought you."

"Why did you then?"

39

"Because I wanted to show you the tomb. I thought you'd be interested. Perhaps I was wrong. Just what does make you tick, Pippa?"

"Oh, you'd like to know, wouldn't you?" she challenged.

"Yes." He had one hand on the ceiling and he stared her straight in the eyes. "But perhaps the Pharaoh's tomb isn't the right place."

He jumped back and banged his left shoulder on the rock. "Ouch!" he gasped.

"Have you hurt yourself?" she said.

"Don't look so anxious. You couldn't care less really."

"That's not fair," she said indignantly.

"Isn't it?" He rubbed his upper arm.

"Here, let me," Pippa said without thinking.

"Do psychologists usually minister to the sick?" he asked dryly as he rubbed the place.

"You can't rub people's minds," she said, kneading his shoulder with her small fingers. "There. That'll stop it bruising."

"Thanks." He smiled. "Come on."

They climbed up towards Ahmed who had seated himself above them during the conversation. How clever the Arab was, Pippa thought, to conserve every bit of energy he had for the climb. They had been travelling upwards in the Pharaoh's tomb along dark, narrow corridors, which were not even four feet in height. That meant most of the time they were bent almost double. It must have been very unpleasant for Rik at six feet two.

Besides the discomfort, he insisted on stopping to show her every detail. He'd been wonderfully enthusiastic about even the precise limestone joints. If she'd been able to straighten up once in a while, she

40

wouldn't have minded. However, Pippa was determined not to show the agony she was in.

"It won't be too long now until we make the King's Chamber will it, Ahmed?"

The Egyptian was still grinning and running easily. Pippa couldn't imagine how he kept it up. She thought if she couldn't stand straight soon and gasp in some fresh oxygen instead of the heavy, stagnant air, she might choke. Suddenly she got just that - wonderful, fresh air.

"Those old Egyptians were great engineers. Thank goodness, a ventilation shaft," Rik said.

They just crouched there, soaking in the air. It was a sign they were near the heart of the pyramid.

"We're metres above ground level," Rik said. "The Pharoah fancied he'd be near the stars."

Pippa gasped in amazement as the entrance corridor finished to reveal the King's Chamber.

"Oh, Rik, look at that tomb." She was so excited she dropped her guard.

"The great granite sarcophagus," he said. "Do you know, Pippa, they'll never be able to move it."

"Why?"

"Because it's one inch wider than the corridor."

She supposed it was a bonus coming along with an archaeologist who knew just about everything.

"It's got no lid," she said in surprise.

"That vanished with the sands of time," he said softly. "That's what I like about this place - it's magical. Those ancient engineers had it all worked out. They just built the pyramid over their king to protect him. It's like putting up a wall about yourself so you can't get hurt."

Pippa glanced at him sharply. Was he getting at her? But the look on his face was reverent. She suddenly realised

41

what an unusual face it was, how sensitive, how intelligent.

In the dawn he had looked like a statue; now, his was the face of a great thinker, of a man so interesting she couldn't take her eyes off him. Suddenly he looked straight at her and, to her amazement, she found herself blushing.

"It's hot, isn't it?" she said to cover her confusion. She glanced at Ahmed then, and he was grinning.

She put out her hand and pressed it on the cold granite. Suddenly Ahmed gave a little whine.

"Don't do that, Pippa," Rik said, "he's superstitious. Some years ago, he wouldn't even come in here."

"Sorry," she said, withdrawing her hand and glancing worriedly at the Egyptian.

"Never mind, you didn't know," Rik reassured her.

Ahmed was in front of them, sidling out into the entrance corridor again.

She and Rik were suddenly alone with the sarcophagus.

"Well," he said, "was it worth it?"

"It was marvellous," she exclaimed. "But I'm sure I'll have backache tomorrow."

"We'll have to see what we can do about that then," he said, a strange gleam coming into his eyes. They were so close that the heat seemed to be rising straight from their bodies. And she was looking up into those eyes, noting their expression, which was suddenly full of tenderness. Pippa was shocked at the feelings which were running through her body and her mind.

How could she get involved with Rik Fenton like this? Why should she even want to? Whatever had happened, *was* happening, between her and Mike, should have made her wary. Pippa couldn't trust her feelings - she knew that. One minute she didn't like Rik, the next she thrilled to him. It was like living with a ball of quicksilver. You lived on the edge, didn't know where you were. And she didn't want to have to face that. She saw too much of it with her patients. She wanted - Pippa tried to think what she really wanted - but her mind was in a daze. The security she'd never had perhaps? It was awful being a psychologist. You knew too much about other people's emotions and nothing about your own.

"What are you thinking?" Rik asked softly. He had his hand on her shoulder.

"I don't know. It's just . . . this place." It was a lame excuse and, in one moment of panic, she knew that he sensed what was the matter. The whole of her mind was telling her that she didn't want to kiss Rik Fenton, but her body was begging for him to go ahead. He did.

With a swift movement, he bent and kissed her cheek, squeezing her shoulder as he did so.

Pippa swallowed. "What was that for?"

"I don't know either. Probably this place," he repeated. His eyes probed hers. "Are you angry?"

She bit her lip, unable to answer, then moved her head back. "I think we should go back now," she said, ignoring the question.

"Is it Mike?"

"Please don't ask," she retorted.

"It is, isn't it?" His lips were set in a stubborn line.

"I don't want to discuss anything now. Please forget it," she said, bending to go under the lintel.

He stopped her. "Don't worry, I will. It's just that you looked . . . sad."

She swallowed again. "Yes." It was all she could say. Her head was reeling from the touch of his lips on her

43

cheek, which still smarted like fire. What was happening to her? What was happening to cool calm Pippa, who never let things get under her skin? Was it Egypt and its strangeness? She just didn't understand how she could switch from one thing to the other like she did. "Please can we go now?"

"Sure thing," he said, following her out. "And. . ." as they straightened, ". . .it won't happen again. I promise."

"Okay," she said, choking inside, thrusting down that small voice in her head which was telling her she'd die if it didn't.

* * *

CHAPTER 4

Pippa sat down to rest outside, feeling as insignificant as an insect with the great pyramid towering above her. She breathed in deeply.

"I am glad to be out," she said, "but it was a wonderful experience."

"Good," he replied, smiling warmly. She was finding Rik a little easier to bear.

"Now let's find the camels." He laughed. His teeth were even and white in his tanned face and Pippa found herself warming to him.

The little Egyptian was waiting for them silently. He pointed to the camels that had brought them the last part of the way.

"What's the matter with him?" Pippa asked.

Rik shrugged then spoke to him in rapid dialect. "Don't take any notice, Pippa. He's just on about bad luck."

"Is it my fault?"

"I told you not to take any notice," Rik insisted, but Pippa saw the frown across his face.

The animals looked even surlier than Ahmed. They gazed at their passengers disdainfully from great lazy-lidded eyes. When the drivers touched them, they spat and grunted.

"Up you go," Rik said as the camel kneeled obediently to let her on.

"I don't really want to," Pippa said, remembering their journey there.

"It isn't that far to the taxis," Rik said as the camel rose to its feet like the stately ship of the desert it was.

Pippa lurched forward clinging on as the driver prodded it on its way. The last thing she heard, as the animal swayed off, was Rik's resonant laughter . . .

Later, when she sank into the back of the taxi, her legs were aching. She turned to Rik. "I heard you laughing," she accused.

"Oh, I'm sorry, but I couldn't help it." She could feel the warmth of his body next to hers. "You did look extremely funny."

Pippa tried to look offended. "Did I? Well, camels aren't the most comfortable form of transport I've ever used. I could barely stay upright." They both laughed then. "But I've really enjoyed today. Thank you, Rik," she added honestly.

"I'm glad." He grinned, and she thought how the smile changed his face. It suited him. "We'll have to do it another time."

"If my father lets you."

"You're a bit hard on him, you know. He had a lot of work to think of."

She wanted to tell Rik Fenton then that her father needed some time off, that he looked poorly, that she was worried about him. But instead she said, "I'm not hard on him. And don't play the amateur psychologist."

"You're not being very fair. In fact, to put it bluntly. . ."

"As you usually do," she cut in sarcastically.

"You are so big-headed."

"Just who do you think you are, Rik Fenton, calling me names? You hardly know me or anything about me," she replied irritably, staring back as the car carried them away from the site of the pyramids.

"That's right but, remember . . . I know your dad."

"I suppose that's meant to be a compliment." She was twisting his words.

"Your dad can be an absolute pain in the neck sometimes, but most of the time he's great."

"So that's what I am, a pain in the neck?"

She was determined to prolong this stupid argument, but Rik just stared in front of him, silently.

* * *

When he got out of the taxi, Rik was looking worried.

"What's the matter?" she asked, shading her eyes from the sun to look at the frown marking his face.

"Feel the wind?" She nodded. "Sandstorms about."

"Oh?" she said, not understanding the importance of his words.

"I shall have to get back to the site."

"You mean our sight-seeings are over for today?"

"I'm afraid so."

"That's all right with me."

"Right, let's get going then. Ahmed."

The guide had just alighted from another taxi with several other Egyptians. Pippa looked into the man's face. He'd been calm before. Now he seemed perturbed.

"Sir?"

"Sandstorms," Rik said, and Ahmed was nodding. "Come on, let's get going," he repeated. "Come on, Pippa." He took her by the arm. "Back to the jeep."

When they reached the vehicle, Rik swung himself up into the driver's seat. He glanced down at Pippa who was making heavy weather of getting in.

"Do you want a hand?"

"No, thank you. I can manage." She would have been all right but her legs and back ached from the day's exertion. She could feel his eyes upon her as she straddled one leg upwards. She didn't know why she felt so ridiculously self-conscious under his gaze. Trying to suppress a tiny throb of pain, she made it.

"You'll have to get fit," he said. "You should exercise more." Once more, he looked maddeningly cool in that terrible heat.

"Do you think so?"

He must have heard the acid in her voice because he grinned. "Where's that monkey, Ahmed?" He glanced behind. As Pippa expected, Ahmed had jumped in as nimbly as the creature Rik had likened him to.

"Here, sir." The voice was devoid of humour or emotion.

"He's still sulking," Rik said.

"You shouldn't call him names."

"Oh, Ahmed doesn't mind. He likes being reminded of his acrobatic prowess."

"Are you always so rude?" she asked, brushing sand from her trousers.

"Always," was the short reply.

Pippa studied his profile as he accelerated. There was a mocking smile about his mouth, but his eyes were intent and his hands strong and responsible on the wheel as he manoeuvred the jeep in the direction of the camp.

Pippa knew how uncomfortable those next few miles were going to be. She hadn't been brought up as an archaeologist's daughter without being fully aware of how

48

unpleasant isolated sites were. She had been on some where the water had to be carried for miles; where there was no sanitation of any kind, and the animal life was decidedly nasty.

Rik was bringing the jeep to a halt. She looked at his face. There was concern in the expression.

"Ahmed!" he shouted and the Egyptian was standing, pulling the canvas top over. Rik helped him then turned back to the wheel. "Storm's on the way," he said by way of explanation.

It was. Pippa wished it could have been rain and thunder instead of that punishing, blurring sand about them, turning and twisting the air devilishly, sometimes clearing a little so they could begin driving again, then enveloping them in terrible, suffocating mists.

"If we were on a couple of camels, we'd be lying down," Rik said suddenly.

"Aren't you ever serious?" she demanded.

"Not unless I have to be. Life's too short."

"It's horrible," she said as they sat marooned in a dusty world. Suddenly, a noise behind made Pippa's flesh creep. In her fright, she clutched Rik's warm arm.

"Shut up, Ahmed," Fenton said curtly and the man's whining died to a moan.

"What's the matter with him?" Pippa asked, still feeling the warmth of Rik's body next to her.

"He's scared, I suppose. I told you he was superstitious. He thinks it's the sand-devil."

Pippa shivered. Rik clasped his hand over hers which lay on his arm. "Don't worry - it isn't." Her face was red as she saw the grin. She tried to withdraw her hand but unsuccessfully.

"Let me go, please."

"Why? I like it."

"Please, Rik." He was lifting his hand. "Thank you." She sat in silence, while the hot wind howled about them making noises almost as frightening as the ones she'd just heard.

"All right now, Ahmed?" He turned and looked back to where the little man was seated, head bowed. Rik shrugged. "He's probably praying to Allah."

"It's not very nice to laugh at him."

"Do you think I'm laughing?"

"You are, aren't you?"

"No, in fact I feel like praying myself. Heaven knows what this wind's done to the tomb entrance." His voice was bitter.

"It isn't your fault."

"No, but if I'd been able to help your dad we might have been able to save something. Alone, he wouldn't have had a chance. Without Ahmed, the boys would be useless. They believe in the sand-devil as well."

"But there's Mike," Pippa said.

"Oh, yes, Mike." His cutting tone made Pippa wince. She had to fight back somehow.

"Then I suppose it's my fault?"

"No, it isn't." His reply was surprisingly vehement. "I was the one who offered to take you - and I've enjoyed it." He was looking straight into her eyes. "All work and no play, you know . . ."

"It's kind of you to say so." She only wished that she didn't sound so sarcastic. "But I'm afraid my father doesn't believe in play."

"What makes you say that?"

"Well, he didn't want anyone to take me . . ." She broke off, loath to discuss with Rik Fenton how she felt.

50

"Your father is quite an ordinary bloke - when you get to know him. He's brilliant, of course, but . . ."

"Oh, you're extremely perceptive." She didn't want to hear any more. She felt Rik was chiding her for not understanding her own father. She knew, too, how nasty her own tone was.

"Remember," he said, and his voice was just as cold, "I've been with him a long time. He's got a lot of problems."

"And I haven't, I suppose?"

"I don't know anything about your problems," he said, misunderstanding quite skilfully. "In fact, I thought all psychologists were meant to have a deep understanding of the processes of the human mind." The patronising tone was just too much.

"Why don't you just be quiet, Rik? When I want your opinion about my personal life and my profession, I'll ask for it."

He jammed his foot on the brake. "Now, listen, Pippa Adams. Nobody speaks to me like that, either."

"You asked for it. In my profession we're taught to tell the truth - get things out in the open."

"Good," Rik said dangerously. "All right, then. I think your attitude is insufferable. Your father is going through a lot. It's only the work that keeps him going. Anything else is a bonus."

"Do you think I don't know that? Do you think I don't know how he looks? I might have been away for six months, but I want to know what's going on. I want to know why you're all at each other's throats. I'm sure that's no good for his health."

"Not all of us are at each other's throats. . . Mia and I . . ."

"Oh, Mia and you," Pippa repeated acidly.

"That's enough," he said.

51

"No, it isn't enough, Rik Fenton. I'm not just someone who's come out to gawp at the sites. I was born on a site like that one out there. The first thing I remember - do you know what that was? Taking a riddle in my hand and sifting the earth. What sort of memory is that? No, I'm a professional. I cut my teeth on antiquity." The bitterness of her words surprised herself. She could hear her own voice but was powerless to stop it. It seemed someone else was speaking.

"But there's something else the matter with you, Pippa, isn't there? It's Mike Nash. . . It is, isn't it? Did you think I hadn't noticed? I'm no psychologist - just a realist. You're getting all het up because he isn't taking any notice of you. What were you expecting?"

"Look, I've had enough of this, too," Pippa said. "I don't intend to discuss my personal life with you, Rik Fenton. Whatever there is between Mike and me, it's nothing to do with you."

"But it is," Rik said. "Anything that affects the site is something to do with me."

There was silence. He drove on and Pippa smarted under the knowledge that Ahmed had been listening to this in the back. She had certainly let her feelings get the better of her. And that was uncharacteristic.

All of a sudden, Rik looked at her and said, "I'm sorry. I had no right to say any of those things." There was quiet about them. The storm outside had abated like the one inside the jeep. "I'm sorry I lost my temper. It was unlike me." He put out his strong hand again and placed it over hers.

She sat quivering at his touch. "I'm sorry, too," she said. At that she was surprised at herself. After all, he'd only been telling the truth. She and Mike weren't the same people any more.

52

The landscape was almost lunar. Either side of the blue-tinged road stretched miles of flat, brown sands and rocks. She wished she could see the Prussian blue of the great Nile alleviating the starkness that hurt her eyes, but there was only sand on sand.

Rik didn't speak, but swung the jeep on, negotiating great heaps that had drifted on to the deserted road. Ahmed was silent too.

She wished then that Rik would say something, tell her anything, how far it was, or their direction. After the storm, the landscape was unrecognisable. She thought over Rik's words. What was going to happen between her and Mike? What could she do to help her father? Had she been an archaeologist like Rik Fenton, there might have been a way.

As they rounded a great overhanging outcrop of rocks coming out of the shadows, she was deciding she wasn't at all happy with things the way they were. And what did Rik Fenton think of her? Did she care about that?

All of a sudden, she knew she did. The young archaeologist might be arrogant but he seemed honest. And that was a quality Pippa respected most of all. She would have liked his admiration. She remembered their brief kiss in the Pharaoh's burial chamber. What would it be like to be Rik Fenton's girl friend? Or his lover?

Rik's eyes were fixed on his driving; he swore a little as he had to slow down at another heap of sand but, all the time, having him in the driver's seat, gave her that sense of security she had always known she lacked ever since the headmistress had told her that her mother had died so far away . . . Yes, whoever Rik Fenton chose, she would have found a guy to rely on. But who would it be? Mia Gabal?

CHAPTER 5

"There it is. There's the camp." Rik's words broke in on Pippa's reverie. "We'll be there in a few minutes."

"Thank goodness," Pippa breathed. It hadn't been quite the kind of day she would be sorry to finish.

"Let's hope the damage isn't too bad, eh?" Rik's face was grim.

Pippa felt that way, too, because it would make her feel even guiltier if the project had been ruined. As the shacks with their corrugated roofs came into view more clearly, Pippa's heart jumped. It couldn't be too bad if they were still standing. Then she realised that for every small building intact, another was buried.

Rik was peering through the windscreen directly in front at the excavations. Evidently his worst fears were coming true as well. The great mounds were surrounded by lots of workers.

"Well and truly buried," he said dully. "All those mounds - and that storm had to come today. We haven't had one like it for ages."

Pippa stared at the damage with him. What was her father going to do? How was he feeling? She didn't have to wait too long to find out.

She could see the tall, thin form standing outside the

tent. She noticed with a pang that his shoulders drooped dejectedly. He seemed as if all the life had been knocked out of him. Once again, she noticed how white his hair had gone.

Rik glanced at her, then he turned the wheel abruptly to bring the jeep right in front of Professor Adams.

"Thank goodness you made it, Rik. I was worried sick about you. Were you caught in the storm?"

Rik nodded, his lips set in a line. "Never mind us. What about the project?"

Professor Adams shook his head. "Buried. I couldn't do a thing about it. I couldn't get the boys to move - as usual. With you and Ahmed . . ." He broke off.

"Blast." The young man hit the side of the jeep. "If only I'd been here, I might have been able to do something."

Pippa had heard enough. She opened the door of the jeep and climbed out slowly. "Hello, Dad."

"Did you have a good day?"

Pippa's heart went out to him. There he was asking if they'd had a good day and look what had happened here.

"Yes, until now," she said, looking at the remnants of the site around her.

Rik turned to Professor Adams. "Pippa's very tired. We spent the day going up and inside the pyramid. It was tough."

"She'd better get some rest then," he said. "And you, Rik. I've still got several things to see to before we get this mess cleared up. It's no use starting before morning."

"You're right. I'm sorry, John, I wasn't here to help," repeated Rik.

Pippa heard the words of apology with regret. She wanted to say she was sorry too, put her arms round her father and tell him that she wished she could help. But she just stood there dumbly.

"Dad? Where's Mike?"

"He's over there, in the tent."

"Wasn't he able to help you?"

Her father looked at her. "I suppose he did what he could. Actually, I couldn't find him during the storm."

"Couldn't you?" Rik Fenton asked. "And Mia, where was she?"

"She did everything she could. But the workers were terrified. And you couldn't blame them. You know what a superstitious lot they are. Mia and I knew that the sand-devil was going to win."

"Oh, Dad," Pippa said impatiently. "That's ridiculous."

"The sand-devil is very real to them. First of all, they don't believe in what we're doing. They're only doing it for the money. It's really against their religion."

"And what does Mia think of that?" Pippa asked. "She's Egyptian, isn't she?"

"Mia understands. She knows that what I'm doing is protection for the site. It's our research money that's keeping the place going. Otherwise the sand-devil *would* win."

As her father spoke, Pippa watched Mike coming towards them. She had always thought him handsome, but in a different kind of way. Now his thin face was creased into a frown and he looked very put-out, very angry. It seemed that Mike wasn't going to take this lying down. And he ignored her.

"You took your time, Fenton. Where the heck have you been?"

"Where you should have been," Rik retorted.

"That's enough," her father cut in.

Pippa swallowed. The last thing she wanted was to see Mike and Rik Fenton rowing.

"I'm quite all right," she said to Mike. "Really, I am. Rik took good care of me."

"It's not you he's worried about, Pippa, it's the site," Rik said acidly.

"Shut up, Fenton!" Mike snarled. "Of course I was anxious about you, Pippa. And, of course, I worried about all the work we've put in. Ruined."

"Not quite ruined. We'll get it sorted out," Rik replied and there was a hard edge to his voice. "With my help." He strode away.

"Well, I think I'll go to my tent," Pippa said lamely. She didn't know what else to say. She was evidently not wanted here. She had taken up enough of everyone's time already . . .

* * *

Pippa was just about to tie up the cotton shirt she was wearing when she heard footsteps outside her tent. A tall shadow was thrown across the canvas. It was her father.

"Pippa?"

"Just a minute." She buttoned up hurriedly, threw back her hair from her eyes, then she was opening the tent flap and stepping outside.

"I came to tell you that there's soup and bread ready. Not very fine, I'm afraid, but it'll have to do. We're not in the mood for cooking tonight."

When Pippa didn't answer, the professor looked at his daughter. She, in turn, looked up at him with eyes so like her mother's, it made his heart leap. Suddenly, he was remembering her as a little girl.

"Did you manage to have a snooze?" He glanced over at the tangled mosquito nets.

57

"Yes. I feel better now."

"I wish *I* did." The words just slipped out.

"I'm so sorry, Dad," Pippa said sadly. "About the damage. Rik and I should have been with you. It would have made all the difference."

"Never mind."

"But you're so tired, I can tell. Why don't you rest? Give it up for a while. Go into Cairo. Check into a hotel. Leave it to Mike and Rik."

"No, I can't do that," he said irritably. "It's out of the question."

"Why?" Pippa asked, incredulous.

"I have my reasons. The site needs protecting."

"But you've got two really good assistants. Why shouldn't *they* protect it? I know Rik's a bit of a pain . . ."

"Don't, Pippa, don't talk about Fenton like that. I couldn't do without Rik," her father said. "He's been a tower of strength."

Pippa could hardly recognise her feelings at this point. Could she be jealous? How ridiculous. She had always known, she'd even been told, that Rik Fenton was his favourite. The two men had everything in common - a single-minded love of their work - an ability to live under the most awful conditions, yet still be happy following their vocation?

That was something she would have liked for herself - that her father would take her into his confidence, like he'd taken Rik Fenton. But she lived in London, away from all this.

She had never had the opportunity. She'd been sent to boarding school. She was too far away from it. She told herself to stop being so stupid. That her father needed every bit of help that he could get. But where did Mike fit in? Perhaps that was why he'd changed. Perhaps that was why he was so miserable. Perhaps nothing was going right in his life or his career.

"And what about Mike?" she asked. "Doesn't he give you support, too?"

Her father's face was set with weariness. He seemed hesitant; there was something on his mind. "Mike," he said, "he's . . . he's tired."

"Tired?" she repeated. Her father was staring up to where the ink-blue sky sported a million stars. Pippa knew what he meant and what he was not prepared to say. Mike had lost all that enthusiasm which had endeared him to her - and her father wouldn't say it in case it hurt her.

"It's all right, Dad," she added. "I think things might have changed between Mike and me. I was probably rushing in a bit too fast . . . in London, I mean."

"Are you telling me that you and Mike aren't in love any more?"

She knew he was embarrassed - why wouldn't he be when he'd never spoken to his daughter so personally before?

"Probably," was her answer.

She could hardly imagine how several days had changed her attitude. Before she'd left London she'd been desperate to see Mike, and when he treated her so coolly she'd been surprised rather than hurt. Perhaps she'd never really been in love with him after all?

And Rik Fenton . . . she could hardly admit the feelings she had for him. He was so exasperatingly arrogant that he'd managed to overshadow the whole situation. The rivalry between him and Mike was so evident that it had taken the place of any conversation or explanation she could have had with Mike. She spent all her time with Rik, and Mike, though he showed no interest in being with her himself, obviously wasn't pleased.

"I'm glad," her father said and his voice made her jump. She had been so deep in thought she'd forgotten she was standing opposite him. He was smiling.

"That's a strange thing to say, Dad," she said.

"I know, but I never thought Mike was right for you."

That was another strange remark. Perhaps there wouldn't be anyone who was *right* for Pippa.

"Why are we standing out here, Dad?" she said to cover her confusion.

"Well, I was going for a walk," he said. "Up there." He pointed to an outcrop of rock. "I often go up there at night. It looks right across the desert. It gives me a respite from all this. You know, Pippa, sometimes I go up there and think about your mother."

"Oh, Dad." She wanted to put out her arms and hold him. But she couldn't. She hadn't done that since she was a little girl.

There was a look in her father's eyes she hadn't seen for years. Tenderness? Maybe he felt the same? But neither made a move.

"You look worn out," he said. "I think you ought to go back to your tent and have a good rest. Tomorrow we're going to have to start clearing this site. And I'd like your help, Pippa, if you feel like it."

"I'd love that. I hope I remember what to do."

"Of course you do," he said surprisingly. "After all, you've had plenty of practice." It was true. They were growing closer. Maybe they'd be able to talk about old times soon...

She suddenly felt more relaxed than she'd done since she'd come to Egypt. She supposed it was being able to speak with him after such a long time. She was glad.

"Shall I come with you on your walk?" However much she wanted to, she was hoping he'd say no. Her legs ached terribly.

"No, you stay here. I'd rather go by myself."

"Right."

She watched his tall figure striding away from the lights of the camp, towards the great boulders that towered over the landscape. She kept on standing, watching as, occasionally, she saw the outline of his body making its way up the path between the rocks. He was a distant silhouette. Then he disappeared from view.

Pippa was about to turn back into her tent when she heard the eerie sound. The shrill, echoing cry filled her with fear. She felt cold all over, unable to move but, as she collected her thoughts, she heard a grating sound like the movement of an avalanche.

Fearfully, she stared into the dusk, across to where her father's shape had disappeared. There were rivers of boulders and smaller stones rolling madly down the face of the cliff, along the side of and, finally, overwhelming the path her father had taken.

"Dad! Dad!" she screamed and, frantically, began to run in the direction of the shadowy rocks.

Pippa was oblivious to how much her legs hurt. Soon her boots were scrabbling on the rough-hewn stone blocks placed there centuries ago. But, climbing, away from the rock fall, she was cold with horror.

Something terrible must have happened to Dad. Why else would he scream out like that? And she was sure it was her father who'd screamed. He was the only one up there. Pippa's whole world started to disintegrate around her.

There was perspiration pouring down her face as she pushed her way up in the moonlight. She had never thought about fetching help; that she herself might be in danger; that she could slip to the bottom and crash down; or be crushed by more falling stones. All she wanted to do was get up there and find him. How could he have been unlucky enough to go on a walk that very moment?

She climbed on as fast as she could but, suddenly, an exhausted Pippa knew she could go no farther. She stood, gasping, her hand pressed to the sharp stitch stabbing her side. She saw, behind her, the lights of the camp strung out like glow-worms in the dark. Then she could see a small, dark figure in the distance, running madly below across the sands towards the rocks. It must be help.

"Help, help!" she shouted. "There's been an accident!"

The wind whirled her words away but, suddenly, the pale, white face of the enormous moon thrust itself from behind a cloud and, to her horror, she could see, clearly, a dark shape spread-eagled at the bottom of the gully to her right. She clung on, rooted with terror.

"Oh, no. Dad! Dad!" And Pippa's sobs reverberated around that lonely ancient fort, centring on her grief for the motionless form below. Was he dead? She couldn't bear it.

After what seemed an age, a dark figure was standing beside her, face set, agonised, dripping with perspiration.

"What's happened, Pippa? What's happened?"

She could have fallen into Rik Fenton's arms. She was so pleased to see him. She caught hold of him with frantic hands, hung on to him just for strength, and pointed downwards.

"Rik, Dad's fallen. Look. There." She gestured frantically into the dusky Egyptian night.

Rik looked down, then turned and cupping his hands yelled below into the darkness. Pippa could hear excited voices in the distance. "Ahmed, bring the boys. There's been an accident." He held her tight against him. "Okay, okay, Pippa. There, there. The boys are on their way. Don't worry, please. You need to get back to the camp. I don't want you falling too.

"There's no way I can get down to your father alone. I'll have to wait until they bring up the ropes. But you, I must get *you* down." He was cradling her shivering body in his arms.

She hardly knew what she was doing but she reacted defiantly. "I'm not going. I have to know what's happened to Dad."

"Come on," Rik urged. "It's dangerous up here." He disengaged her clinging arms and, expertly, started to guide her down to the safer part of the path. "Now, just sit here and I'll go up again with the boys. I promise you I'll be back to you soon."

"Do you think he's . . ?" The word wouldn't come out. She stared blankly in front of her. She couldn't bear the thought her father might be dead. And they had so much to say to one another. Rik didn't answer, just squeezed her hand tightly.

At that moment, Ahmed and some of the boys appeared, nimbly negotiating the great slabs of rock. Rik straightened as the workers surrounded him, their eyes an eerie white in the moonlight. He smoothed her hair back as her own eyes sought his.

"I'm going to help Ahmed. I'll be back down with the news as soon as I can. I promise you." Gesturing them to hurry, he turned to follow, shouting instructions as he went.

Pippa sat, head in her hands, praying her father was alive. Tears began to stream down her cheeks. Would it be too late to tell Dad how much she cared about him? She suddenly felt very cold in the thin shirt, and sat, hunched up, hugging her knees.

* * *

It seemed ages until she heard Rik shouting, "Pippa, Pippa, he's alive."

She struggled to her feet. "Thank God."

She was straining her eyes into the darkness. Then she could see Rik's white shirt - and the dark shape of the long stretcher on which her father was being carried between two of the boys. When they finally got down to her, she rushed along beside them staring at Professor Adams's still features. He looked dead and he had a dark, swelling bruise and gash on his temple. The rest of his face was scratched and bleeding.

Rik glanced at her sharply. "Honestly, he's just concussed. We have to get him to the hospital."

"Will it take long?" Pippa asked unable to hide her anxiety.

"We'll do our best," Rik said. "I'll drive there in the jeep." All the time, they were clambering down between the boulders, the lights of the camp getting nearer and nearer . . .

* * *

Pippa stood aside helplessly as Rik and the native workers struggled to get her unconscious father into the back of the jeep. The professor's face was grey except for those grazes on the left side of his face and the bright searing gash and bruise above his temple.

She put her hand on the side of the vehicle to steady herself. She felt sick and disorientated. Then someone else was standing, silently, beside her.

"Mike?" she said, looking up.

His face was drawn and haggard. "What on earth happened?" he asked in a flat voice.

Rik Fenton turned. "Well, where were you?"

"Dad fell from the rocks," Pippa cried. The last thing she wanted now was an argument between Rik and Mike. She couldn't stand it.

"I was asleep in my tent. I can't believe I didn't hear anything. How is he?" Mike was peering into the back of the jeep.

"Concussed," Pippa said. She could see Rik's lips set in a grim line. He wasn't going to drive after all; he was leaving that to Ahmed, who was crouched over the wheel.

"Get on the radio, Nash, and let the hospital know what's happened so they'll be ready. Come on, Pippa," Rik said. He was extending his hand. Pippa took it and pulled herself into the jeep.

"Pippa," Mike was saying, "you look awful. Won't you stay here and get some rest? I'll go instead."

"No, I'm going with Dad!" Pippa cried as Ahmed turned the key in the ignition.

The powerful engine sprung into life. Rik was steadying her as the jeep lurched forward over the sand, leaving Mike standing, silhouetted in the moonlight far behind.

As Ahmed drove swiftly as the sand-devil in the direction of Cairo, the two of them crouched over Professor Adams.

Pippa stared into her unconscious father's face. Then she looked up at Rik.

"What am I going to do without him?"

"You won't have to do without him," Rik said softly, tilting her head up till their eyes met. "No, he's going to be all right."

"How do you know?" she asked, her eyes brimming with tears.

"I can feel it in my bones. Call it a sixth sense. The fates wouldn't allow it. Besides, we're going to take him to the university hospital. It's a wonderful place." His words were certainly comforting.

"What do you mean, the fates?" He shook his head at her question, then patted her on the shoulder. She was glad of his hand.

"I mean the fates are supposed to be cruel, but they've always been good to me. They brought me out here - to your father and to this job. They won't give up on me now. And, besides, they owe us one. After burying the tomb."

Rik Fenton leaned back against the canvas cover of the jeep. He suddenly looked very tired. There seemed to be nothing else to say to each other as the vehicle bumped on and on interminably, along the road to Cairo. Pippa hadn't meant to cry but, suddenly, those tears that had been stinging her eyes began to run down her cheeks.

"Don't cry, Pippa. He's going to be all right," Rik repeated.

"I hope so." And there was heartbreak in her tone. He was looking straight into her eyes. She recognised the kind of warmth and understanding she thought she'd once seen in Mike's. She had never believed she'd see it in Rik Fenton's. As she looked away from him she felt a tiny throb inside, an imperceptible reaching out towards him. But he was looking into her father's face.

"Get a move on, Ahmed," he shouted. "We've got to get the professor to the hospital. Quickly!" Then he was bending and cradling Professor Fenton to shield his injured body from the jolts of that punishing journey.

Ahmed cruised along the highway, on and on towards the dazzling neon lights of Cairo. As they approached, Pippa never even noticed the sky scrapers, their twinkling lights seeming to stretch endlessly into the dark sky; nor the floodlit mosques and minarets. All she could think of was getting her father to the hospital in time.

"Not long now," Rik said as Ahmed swung the jeep to left and right, taking turnings, revving up, slowing down in the heavy night traffic. "Thank goodness it's not rush hour." It was bad enough.

Pippa was so glad that Rik was with her. All the animosity of the day before seemed forgotten. There was warm contact between them and she was grateful for the way he looked after Dad.

Rik's arrogance had been replaced by a softness she could hardly believe he possessed. He was certainly a man of contrasts. She was learning a lot about Rik Fenton and the more she saw, the more she liked. But she had no time to think of that now - only the tall, thin frame which was lying between them. Soon they had reached Roda Island, on which the hospital stood.

"Sir, sir, hospital, sir," Ahmed was jabbering and pointing. Rik was already getting things together in preparation for moving the professor as they swung through the gates. They came to a juddering stop and Pippa was stretching up and out, looking around wildly for help. When it came, she and Rik were running alongside the stretcher as the white-coated men wheeled Professor Adams through to the emergency area.

Rik took over immediately. Pippa was glad and sank down on one of a line of hard, red chairs positioned outside a cubicle. She knew she would never be able to get through this alone.

They took her in to see her father later. He was lying motionless beneath a shaded light in a small, white room. Rik and she stood and watched him for what seemed a very long time. Professor Fenton had been through thorough hi-tech examinations and now they were waiting for the results of some tests.

"How bad will it be, Rik, do you think, if his skull's fractured?" It was a stupid question to ask. She just said it for something to say. He shook his head, stroking her shoulder to calm her.

"Come on, Pippa, it's no use you thinking like that. There's nothing you or I can do. It's up to them now. What you need is a rest."

"I can't leave him," she protested, but he was leading her from the room. "I have to stay in the hospital."

"You know what I'm going to do?" Rik asked. "I'm going to get you back to a hotel. It's a good one and it's only a stone's throw from here. I'll stay with your father. You're going to sleep and, if there's any news, I'll call you immediately."

"No, Rik, I have to stay."

"Don't you trust me?"

"Of course I do, but . . ."

"No buts. There's absolutely nothing you can do. This is an excellent hospital. We just have to leave it to the professionals. If you crack up, then it'll make things worse for your father."

He was talking sense and she knew it. And she did trust him to phone her. With one last look at her father's almost unrecognisable face, wired up as he was to all kinds of technical equipment, she returned to Rik and walked down the corridor with him, his arm about her.

* * *

CHAPTER 6

They didn't speak then, not even when they were in the jeep. She sat silently beside him as he drove down the road and turned left about three hundred metres from the hospital area.

"Here we are. Pippa, it would be sensible to try and get some sleep." He was looking at her earnestly. "It's almost the only thing you can do to help yourself and him."

The bright street lights were masking the dawn. Pippa hadn't noticed the redness of the sky and the creeping approach of morning. She had imagined herself watching an Egyptian dawn, but not like this. She staggered a little.

"Hey, you're nearly asleep," he said. Supporting her with his arms, he took her through the doors. Instead of protesting, she stood, his broad frame almost holding her up, as he made the reservation. When the porter arrived to take her upstairs, Rik said, "All right, I'm coming, too."

When they were in the lift, she looked up at him. "I'm sorry."

"Don't be."

"You must be exhausted yourself."

He shook his head imperceptibly. "I'm used to it."

"You mean, I'm a woman and that's different."

Her prompt reply signalled to Pippa that she was suddenly coming out of the shock of the accident. He made no response to her feeble quip.

Just then the lift stopped and the door slid open. The porter, who was going ahead of them along the corridor, stopped outside a door. "Your room, miss."

"Thanks." Rik inserted the key card and, as he held open the door, Pippa walked unsteadily into the room.

"I'll be all right now, Rik." He didn't answer, but just tipped the Egyptian, who was waiting respectfully. The man withdrew. Then Rik took a good look around.

"Right, it looks okay. I suggest, by the look of you, you get into bed and just sleep."

He opened the buttoned pocket of his jacket, withdrawing a small book. He wrote something down and handed it to her.

"The hospital number. Ring and I'll be on the other end. And, don't worry, Pippa. I'll look after him for you."

She could have kissed him then. He must have sensed it because, suddenly, he was planting a kiss lightly on both cheeks.

"Thank you, Rik, for everything. What would I have done without you?" She passed a hand over her forehead. She was shaken and confused.

"I was only there, that's all. That's my function. Clearing up." It was a remark which showed Pippa that Rik too was taking himself in hand. "Just trust me, Pippa. And I'll ring as soon as there's anything to report."

She sighed and collapsed on a settee. "I'll be back at the hospital soon. After I've slept. I am tired."

"You look it. I should run a bath as well and have a good soak. You know what you said in the lift . . ." She

71

couldn't remember, and was puzzled. ". . . about a woman being different?" He was smiling. "I have noticed . . . and I definitely like it. Good-night."

"Goodbye, Rik." She allowed him to let himself out. Then she got up and walked over to the bed wearily and lay there, not even wanting to take off her clothes

* * *

Pippa was still lying on the counterpane fully clothed when she came to. She could hardly remember what had happened but the awful memory soon returned. Her sleep hadn't been that good, although it had been deep. She'd tossed and turned, her head full of confused dreams.

She controlled an impulse to run to the telephone and find out what was happening to her father. She felt stiff and dirty. No wonder. She looked down at her clothes - she needed a bath. Then she blinked at the time. It was noon. Heaven knows what had happened by now.

She began to tear off her clothes and made for the bathroom. It was then that she remembered she hadn't brought anything else to wear. Everything had happened too quickly. All she had with her was her handbag. She'd picked it up automatically before climbing into the jeep, otherwise she wouldn't have had that with her either. She just wished she'd had time to bring a change of clothes as well.

But did any of it matter? Her father was lying unconscious in the hospital and she had to get down there quickly.

She was still wrapped in towels when she rang the hospital to find out about her father.

"How is Professor Adams?"

72

"Who is speaking, please?"

"His daughter. I'm staying at the Saladin Hotel."

"I'm putting you through."

The wait was an agony. When the nurse replied, Pippa was nervously twisting a strand of her long, fair hair about in her fingers.

"Professor Adams is as well as can be expected, but I'm afraid he has not regained consciousness. Do you wish to speak to Mr. Fenton?"

"No, thank you, I'll be over directly." Pippa felt shaky as she replaced the receiver. Somehow she had to face what was happening, to think of all the things she hadn't had time to think of last night. But she had to get down there - whatever happened she was going to spend some time with her father now.

A moment later the phone rang, making her jump. She picked it up and now her hand was trembling. Perhaps they hadn't told her everything?

"Hello?" she said in a small voice.

"Rik here."

She was full of relief when she heard the deep tone of his voice.

"I've just telephoned the hospital."

"I know, the nurse just told me. I was dozing outside the door."

"You've been there ever since?"

"I told you I would be."

"I know and, Rik . . . thank you."

"No trouble. I'm just as worried about him as you are. But," he added hastily, "there hasn't been any change. At least they haven't said he's any worse. Did you sleep well?"

"Yes," she lied, thinking about all those troubled dreams.

"And you feel better?"

"Yes."

"Good, then I'll come over and fetch you."

"Rik?" Her voice was still a little shaky. "Do you think that he's really going to be all right?"

"Don't think about it. Let's just wait and see." Rik's voice was, as usual, strong and comforting. "I won't be long, Pippa. You get ready. OK?"

"Goodbye, Rik. See you soon."

She quickly changed into her clothes from yesterday. It was only when she was getting ready to leave that she thought about Mike. He had been close to her before, now she hadn't even noticed he wasn't there.

And, now, Rik Fenton had been everything to her. She'd relied on him utterly and completely. She remembered what her father had said before the accident, that he couldn't do without Rik Fenton. She understood what he'd meant. She would never have been able to cope. Whether she was a psychologist or not. It was only when something happened like this, that you knew who you could rely on.

Her job in London was totally demanding. All the men she came in contact with were either fellow psychologists, doctors or psychiatrists, who were all too busy dealing with patients to lend any real support to a colleague.

Besides, she'd never really needed anyone before. Not seriously anyway. In fact, as she thought about it, the last time she really needed someone was after her mother's death. There hadn't been anybody there for her except her friends and the nuns in the school. Now someone had turned up at the right moment. It just happened to be Rik Fenton. He had been able to take care of everything. A few days ago, she would have resented it because she had never seen herself as a girl who needed a man to lean on. She was too self-sufficient and aware of the world.

At least, that's what she'd imagined. In fact, Rik was the kind of man who'd always annoyed her immensely with his arrogance and air of command. She'd never been keen on men, who reeked of self-importance.

She thought now that she'd probably chosen Mike because he was quiet, even secretive. But Rik Fenton had a power about him that diminished others, and she had never liked that before. He knew a lot and he liked everyone around him to know. As she picked up her bag, Pippa found herself thinking more and more of Rik, realising her first impression of him had been wrong.

A moment later, there came a knock on the door.

"Hang on, Rik, just a moment."

She hurried across the room and opened the door but, instead of Rik, she was confronted by a dark man in a black suit, a stern-looking woman and, beside them, a smiling and apologetic desk manager.

"Miss Adams, I am very sorry but this gentleman would like to talk to you."

The dark man was reaching in his breast pocket and holding something out to her. It looked like a police badge.

"Who are you?" She was at a loss, and swallowed, looking from one to the other. "Has something happened to my father? Have you come from the hospital?"

"No, Miss Adams, that's not the reason. But I am a policeman. I would like to have a few words with you."

"I don't understand."

"The accident."

She looked at him and relief flooded over her. "Of course, the accident. Oh, do come in, but what do you want to

75

know?" She was looking from the man to the woman. And the desk manager was bowing and withdrawing.

"Inspector Marat." The policeman held out his hand. He was tall, for an Egyptian, and had a prominent nose and quick, bright eyes, which appeared to be looking everywhere inside the room. "And this is my colleague, Angie Dura."

"Hello," Pippa said evenly, impatient to get to the hospital. "Would you like to sit down? How can I help you?"

The policewoman was taking a book from her bag and a gold pen.

"You can imagine that we would like to ask you a few questions, Miss Adams, about the accident," the inspector began.

Pippa sat down, too, facing them. "Who reported it?"

"Actually, it was a Mr. Fenton."

"Rik?"

"Yes, Rik Fenton. He's very well known. And, of course he was right. And, anyway, if there has been an injury like that, our men would have found out from the hospital. As in your country, all accidents are reported."

"Well, I wish I could help you. As far as I know, my father just slipped down the gully. One moment I could see him, the next he disappeared. And then I heard him scream. I think it was some kind of avalanche. Stones. And that's all I know. Did you see the doctor's report?"

"Yes, but. . ." The inspector hesitated and, at that moment, Pippa wished Rik would appear. ". . . but we would like *you* to tell us exactly what happened."

"Why? Is there any doubt about what I've said? My father fell. I don't know how."

"But we do."

76

"Then why are you questioning me?" Pippa queried. "I have to get down to the hospital and see how he is. If you've been to the site and looked already, then you know. I don't see how I can add to that."

"I'm afraid it's not quite as simple as that," Inspector Marat said. "Your father was very used to that path. And he may not have slipped."

Pippa drew in her breath. She couldn't believe what the man was suggesting.

"What do you mean?"

"His fall was rather too violent. And he has some other injuries. There is a possibility . . ." the inspector paused, and the woman stopped scribbling and looked at Pippa, ". . . it's possible that someone else was responsible for your father's fall into the gully. Also he had sustained a blow to the *back* of the head."

"You don't mean it?" Pippa cried.

"I'm afraid we do, Miss Adams," the inspector said. "And you, naturally, were the person to whom he was talking before he climbed the rocks. But, I would like you to go over the details again. Slowly, please."

"I've just told you what happened," Pippa said.

"The details, Miss Adams, please?" the inspector insisted.

"You mean about Dad and me?" The two of them were nodding. "Why do you want to know?"

"Carry on, Dura."

The policewoman produced a clip-board and, looking carefully at Pippa, began to read in a colourless voice.

"I heard the professor and his daughter. Their voices were raised. I thought they seemed to be quarrelling . . ."

"Stop!" Pippa cried. "What's this all about?"

"I'm afraid, Miss Adams, that there is someone on the

site who was quite ready to give us a statement about last night."

"Who?" she said. "It's preposterous. Do you think I had something to do with my father falling? I can't believe this."

"All we want is your version," the policewoman said.

"Version?" It was getting more like a crime film. "What exactly am I supposed to have done?"

"How can we tell you anything, Miss Adams, until you tell us?" The inspector was smiling.

"Do you suspect me of pushing my father?"

"Who said anything about *pushing*?" Inspector Marat replied, leaning back in the chair patiently.

Pippa just stared at them. Suddenly, there was a terse knocking at the door.

"Thank goodness, Rik." She ran across to the door. "Rik, come on, the police are here."

Inspector Marat was getting to his feet as Rik strode in. "What's all this?"

"They think I had something to do with Dad's fall," Pippa said indignantly.

"What on earth are you doing here, Marat?" Rik asked.

The police inspector shrugged and sighed. "We have to make our enquiries, Mr. Fenton. And Miss. Adams was the last one to see the professor safe and sound. These inquiries are just routine."

"Just what is going on, man? Don't you think Miss. Adams has enough on her plate with the professor lying unconscious?"

"Yes, but we still have to make our inquiries. I believe you know that, when there have been accusations, we have no option but to investigate. You should know that, Mr. Fenton. Remember . . ."

"Yes, Marat, that will do. So what's this about accusations?"

Pippa was trembling when Marat finished.

"Don't worry," Rik said to her, "everything's going to be fine."

"They think I pushed him, Rik." She stared at the inspector. "You do, don't you?" she cried. She rushed over to the settee and sat down.

The policeman shrugged. Pippa couldn't believe it.

"Now calm down, Pippa," Rik said quietly, going over to her and sitting on the arm. "Leave this to me. I understand these people."

He turned to Marat. "You haven't told us, Marat, have you - who gave you that statement? But I bet it was Ahmed. It was Ahmed who came to you, wasn't it?"

He stared at the inspector before continuing. "Now I've some news for you. Our little foreman has taken a very strong dislike to Miss Adams here. All because she put her hand on a sarcophagus without knowing. We were climbing inside one of the pyramids yesterday, and he was with us.

"He's convinced she's a perfect Jonah and I know he thinks the professor's accident was her fault as well. According to Ahmed and the workers, Pippa is bad news. You know how superstitious the workmen are when they are excavating, Marat?"

To Pippa's relief, the inspector was nodding in agreement.

"Anyway, I can put your mind at rest," Rik added. "I saw everything. I was there, walking round the tents when the two of them were having the conversation. They were not quarrelling. Pippa was talking quite normally with her father. She didn't go on the outcrop of rocks with him, because I saw her watching him as he went.

"The old boy's a venturesome devil. He does it every night and I've told him not to. At least, I tried to warn him, but Professor Adams, as you know also, Marat, is a very stubborn man. If somebody did push him, it wasn't Pippa. The whole idea is just ridiculous. She's come over here to Egypt to be with him." Rik opened his hands in a helpless gesture.

"I realise you have to make your enquiries, but it's going a bit too far. Now, can you leave the girl alone? And wait until I get hold of Ahmed."

The inspector was nodding. The policewoman was putting her notebook away. He looked less inquisitive and more approachable.

"Well, Mr. Fenton, if you say so. I think by now we can trust each other. Naturally, we have no desire to upset Miss. Adams in the circumstances."

He turned to Pippa. "I'm very sorry about your father. He is a good man. A great man and many Egyptians admire him. In Egypt, we're not particularly fond of foreign archaeologists, but your father treats our treasures with reverence."

Pippa swallowed. Then Marat was turning to Rik again.

"Perhaps I'm the one who should talk to Ahmed."

"No, I will," Rik said. "We don't want any more trouble with him. He and I understand one another. And we have to start clearing the site. If the boys get upset the whole thing will be off."

They were looking at each other in a strange way. Then the inspector smiled and the tension in the atmosphere was broken.

"Once again, my apologies for this very unpleasant

intrusion, Miss Adams. Come on, Dura - and, Mr. Fenton, I'll be expecting you at the station to verify this in a statement. Good-morning."

Pippa closed her eyes in relief as they let themselves out. "Rik, what a nightmare," she burst out.

"It's best to keep on the good side of them," he said. "They're all right if you do. Otherwise . . . come on, cheer up." His eyes were smiling at her. "At least I saved you from rotting in an Egyptian jail."

"Oh, stop it, Rik. Why did Ahmed do it?"

"Ahmed can be singularly vicious," Rik replied, "but don't take it to heart. That's the kind of guy he is."

"I must really have got under his skin," she said.

Rik didn't answer. Then, in a moment, he looked into her eyes. "I think you're destined to get under a lot of people's skin, Pippa. Come on. Let's go and see your dad."

He was taking her arm, so she bent, picked up her bag and left the room.

* * *

CHAPTER 7

When they got to the hospital, Rik Fenton stopped outside the door of her father's room.

"Aren't you coming in?" she said.

"Of course I am. But later. I've a lot of things to see to. I'll be back."

"Goodbye," she said, her unwilling hand resting on the door handle, watching Rik Fenton walk away. She realised just how much she wanted him to be with her but, of course, he couldn't. Not all the time.

Pippa sat beside her father's bed for a good two hours. Professor Adams never moved, just lay still and white as death. She knew she would never forget that time of soul-searching; of watching her father, lying so far from the normal world. She had so much time to say under her breath all those things she'd wanted to say to him for years, but he couldn't hear her. He was asleep, suspended in time. Occasionally, she leaned over him and talked to him; said things she was sure he'd like to hear, but he remained motionless, death-like.

When she could stand no more, she wandered over to the window and stared across the city. To think she'd come all the way to Egypt to see him, to be near him; and perhaps now she would never be able to.

She would have liked to have sat down and howled. Outside, life was just going on; in that still hospital room it seemed to have stopped.

Around her was the hum of a mighty city but, somewhere in the distance, the great pyramids were still standing surrounded by rolling acres of never-ending sand. That desert where the sand-devil whirled and danced his way over the graves of kings. She didn't want to leave her father here. It was not his home.

She sighed trying to shake off the horrible feeling of depression that would not go away. Then she wandered in again and looked at her father, then out to the small restaurant to take some juice and rolls because, now, for the first time, she found a need to eat.

There were other visitors sitting, hunched in silence. She wondered miserably where Rik was and decided that when he came again, she'd ask him to go with her to see the doctor again.

She finished her meal and walked back along the corridor towards her father's room. She primed herself to believe he'd regain consciousness soon; she had to, so she could keep going herself. As she approached the door, she was surprised to find it was ajar. She hesitated, then, putting out her hand gently, she pushed it open.

Two figures were standing by his bed, their backs to her. A slim, dark woman had her head nestled into the hollow of Rik Fenton's shoulder. He had his arm about her. A tiny throb ran through Pippa which she didn't recognise immediately. She assumed it was surprise. Afterwards, she recognised it as a reaction to seeing a woman in Rik's arms.

Mia Gabal and Rik. Ever since her dream it had seemed a possibility.

Pippa hung back. There was something so intimate in the way they were standing that she didn't feel
she could just walk in. And that strange feeling was still
with her. She'd been so stupid to think Rik Fenton's time
was solely taken up by her. It stood to sense that he had
someone to be with. She remembered the way he had
held Dr. Gabal's hand when he had introduced her.

Suddenly Pippa felt she had no right standing
watching such a personal scene. Mia was raising her
head and looking into Rik's face. And he stood, brushing
something from her cheek. Pippa took one tiny step
backwards. She'd return when they'd finished. But they'd
heard her already.

"Pippa," Mia Gabal said. "I'm so pleased to see you
again." She broke away from Rik, who stood smiling. She
kissed Pippa on both cheeks then, putting an arm about
her shoulders, drew her to the bed. They stood in silence,
looking at Professor Adams.

"I was so upset when I heard, Pippa," Mia Gabal said.
"It's a terrible thing to happen. But I'm sure he's going to
be all right. I'm sure the tests will show . . ."

"Do you know which ones he's had?" Pippa asked.

"No, but I should think they will take some time.
Neurosurgery is a very precise science."

"Like archaeology," Rik said, making a little open-
handed gesture. "I know, you two stay here and I'll go and
see if there's any news."

"No, I'm coming too," Pippa cried.

"Will you be all right, Mia?" Rik asked.

Mia Gabal nodded. "Oh, yes, I want to stay with him."

"Right, we'll be back in a minute. Come on, Pippa."

The two of them walked through the door, leaving Mia
holding Professor Adams's hand.

"She's a very nice woman," Rik said as they walked down the corridor.

"I can see that," Pippa said desperately. She was behaving in a very silly way; not wanting Rik Fenton to know she cared he had a girlfriend, not wanting him to think she was entirely selfish.

"You should get to know her, you know," he continued. "Mia is a very great friend of ours."

"*Ours*?" she repeated.

"Your father and myself."

"I'm sure she is," Pippa said thinking of how they were standing.

"You know, when I first came out to Egypt, Mia was already working with your dad. I admire her a great deal."

"So you've known her quite a long time?"

"Yes, she's been a wonderful friend to us all. When your father . . ." Rik suddenly broke off.

"Yes?" Why didn't he finish the sentence? What was he going to say about Mia and her father?

"I think you should talk to her yourself," Rik said. "Anyway, what's all this deep questioning? I thought you had a good chat that night you went out in the desert with her and Mike. I suppose your profession is to blame. Always wanting answers, and when you can't get them straight away then you fabricate some sort of theory."

Pippa was amazed. His remark was quite uncalled for. "That's not fair. What do you know about psychology anyway? It's a very precise science." She knew she was mimicking the words he'd just uttered. And her voice raised a little.

"Look, Pippa, I know you've had a shock, but I'm sure everything's going to be all right. Let's get over to the

85

doctor and see what he says." He thought she was worried about her father, not about him.

"Look, Rik, there's nothing wrong with me."

"Isn't there? What I was trying to say in my clumsy way was that it's doing neither of us any good standing here quarrelling. What is eating you anyway? You'd do much better to leave Mia with him for a bit. You've been at it for two hours already. And there's nothing worse than you just sitting there endlessly."

Pippa didn't know how he could change so suddenly. Three or four hours ago she'd been glad of his keen perception, now he seemed intent on patronising her.

"Rik," Pippa interrupted, standing quite still, "I shall spend exactly as long as I want with my father. I'd be really pleased if you'd stop telling me what to do."

"Well," he said. His face was extremely serious, "You know what I think, Pippa. I think that however much you want to be with your father all the time, you're not up to it. That it would be much better to let someone else stay with him for a while. Like Mia, for instance. Why won't she do?"

"You really are the limit, Rik. There you go again saying what I should or should not do. I'll do what I want. Of course I'm grateful to you for last night and for this morning, but I . . ."

"Oh, don't be grateful. I wanted to do it. But I can't work you out, Pippa. Just what is up with you? It couldn't be because Mia and I were in there together, could it?"

It was the first time for years that Pippa felt herself really blushing. He was staring at her. He put back his head and laughed. He was so insensitive.

"I don't believe it," he said. "You're angry because Mia and I were there with your father and you weren't. That's

86

it, isn't it? You might be his daughter, Pippa, but we're his *friends*. Mia has as much right to be with him as anyone else. I'm getting fed up with you, Pippa, and your jumping to conclusions. When you're capable of making reasonable assumptions, I'll be back. *And not until then.*"

He looked angrier than he'd been in the jeep when they'd had an argument coming back from the pyramids. Pippa suddenly realised he had as bad a temper as she did. But this time he wasn't cooling as he'd done in the jeep during the sandstorm. She also noticed the dark rings under his eyes again. He looked worn-out. Perhaps neither of them were thinking clearly?

He stood threateningly for a moment, and then he turned off and strode down the corridor. Pippa watched him go, her hands clenched by her sides and her eyes sparkling. But, inside, she was very angry with herself for provoking the scene; she was also ashamed because her father was lying in there unconscious.

She didn't hear the footsteps approaching. "I am afraid Rik has rather a temper," Mia Gabal said.

Pippa swung round and the Egyptian laid a calm hand upon her arm. "Please let me apologise for Rik. He can be very hasty . . . but only when he's worried. And he is worried about your father. He cares for him a lot."

Mia let go of Pippa's arm and took off her spectacles. She rubbed her forehead with her hand and sighed wearily. "Forgive me, Pippa, but I'm very tired. As soon as I heard about the accident I got over here as quickly as I could. You know, I live to the west of the city and it takes a bit of time."

She put on her glasses again. Pippa could see her eyes were very bright, very bright indeed. She was on the point of crying. "Please come in and see your father. This has

87

all been a terrible shock. Let's go in together and sit by him."

Pippa allowed herself to be taken by the arm and the two of them walked back to her father's room. Neither spoke, as each was lost in their own private thoughts. Once, inside, Mia pulled up a chair for Pippa next to her father and then sat down beside her.

Occasionally, Mia laid a hand on Pippa's arm to soothe her and smiled. She was, as Rik said, a very nice woman. If it hadn't been for Pippa's foolish fears, she would have found her presence comforting. However, the two women sat together for an hour in what could be taken for a companionable silence.

And, three hours later, when Rik had taken over and Mia and Pippa had gone to have a rest, Professor Adams opened his eyes, stared around uncertainly then, looking at Rik Fenton bending over his bed, gave his young assistant a slight smile of recognition.

* * *

CHAPTER 8

Two days later, Pippa knew what her father had meant when he'd said he couldn't do without Fenton. Neither could he do without Mia. The two of them seemed invincible. They had complete control. And he was happy to let them do everything. On account of the concussion, her father had to keep very quiet and to stay under observation; there seemed no chance of him getting out of hospital for a while.

Mike had turned up eventually. Pippa was sitting alone at the small table in the room adjoining her father's. She looked up. "Mike." She got up, thinking he'd take her in his arms. She'd spent quite a lot of time wondering about their relationship. It was no good thinking of Rik any more. He and Mia Gabal were evidently close. Not that she'd seen them doing anything. It was just the way they were. Any woman would recognise the signs.

But Mike wasn't interested in her either. He avoided her and stared into the next room. "I should have come before but someone had to look after the site with Fenton and Gabal here all the time. I've been trying to clear the remnants of the sandstorm."

The way he said it told Pippa he blamed everyone for the disaster except himself. The last thing she wanted then was him whining and complaining. Never mind the site. What about her father? When Pippa looked in his face, she felt she hardly knew him. He seemed unapproachable and morose.

"I'm sure Dad'll be pleased to hear that, Mike, when he's better," she replied evenly. "Luckily, things are going well with him. I thought you'd like to know."

Later, Mike was particularly rude to Rik and Mia. He took the opportunity to be awkward whenever he could and Pippa was almost sure she recognised the reason. He was jealous of the influence they had on her father.

And it wasn't true he was doing all the work on the site. Mia, Rik and she were travelling up and down all the time. Yes, Mike was a different man these days, and Pippa certainly didn't like it. There was no way their relationship would take off again.

* * *

"This hasn't been much of a holiday for you, Pippa, has it?" Mike said one afternoon a week or so after her father had regained consciousness. He had approached her quite casually where she was seated, carefully sifting through some broken remnants of pottery.

She looked up at him, his frame blocking out the sun. She felt particularly alone because Rik and Mia were busy as usual, and the sifting was getting extremely tedious.

"No, I suppose it hasn't but, at least Dad's getting better," she replied. "Anyway I shall be able to help here before I go back to London. I've extended my leave actually." She glanced briefly at Mike.

Once, he would have been wildly happy about that.

"You know, before the accident, Dad said he'd like my help. It's the least I can do. If the tests go well this afternoon, he may be back on his feet pretty soon, as long as he's careful."

She was glad to have a few hours off hospital visiting while her father was up at the doctors, and she had driven out to the site, as usual, to see if she could help with the clearance.

She looked over to where Mia and Rik were standing outside a neighbouring tent, poring over a site map. Mike was looking in their direction as well.

"Make a good team, don't they?" he said. His tone was flat.

"Yes, they know what they're doing."

"You can say that again." Mike put both hands on his pockets and stood, staring across the desert to the outcrop of rocks. Then he stared at her, "In fact, I could say I'm a little worried about what they *are* doing."

"What?"

He sat down on the vacant canvas chair. "Pippa, I came out here to be your father's chief assistant. Once Fenton was on the dig, things changed." Mike cleared his throat. He seemed to be having some difficulty with what he intended to say.

"You can tell me, Mike." Pippa hoped she didn't seem too eager. Was she about to find what had caused the real animosity between the three of them?

"He, and Gabal, of course, seemed to be taking over more and more."

"And you feel cut out?"

"No, it's not personal." He was hesitating again. "But I suppose I shouldn't be saying this to you about your father. You are his daughter, and it could upset you."

"What about Dad?" She couldn't see Mike's eyes behind his sunglasses.

"Have you ever wondered what really happened up there?" He gestured in the direction of the Roman fortifications. "I think you have, Pippa, and so have the police." She didn't want to remember Inspector Marat's visit to her hotel room. "And, I believe, they're still making investigations."

"How do you know?"

"All I know is that they are still not convinced it was just an accident."

"I don't see what you're getting at." He was looking across at Rik and Mia again.

"Well, I don't know *what* I'm getting at really. It just seems so strange how he could *fall*. He was used to that walk."

"Come on, Mike, what do you mean?" Pippa wasn't sure if Mike knew anything else about the fall. Did he know for instance about her father's injury to the back of the head? And what about Ahmed? Surely he'd heard about Rik speaking to the man? But she couldn't be sure. So she added innocently, "Surely you don't think Rik or Mia had anything to do with it?"

"I never said that." He was hesitating again. "Mia is an Egyptian. There are many Egyptians, who are dead against any kind of archaeological excavations carried out by foreigners. Who knows?"

There was no mistaking Mike's implications. He was indirectly accusing Mia of complicity.

"Well, I think you're going too far, Mike," defended Pippa, although her stomach was giving tight little turns. "As far as I can see, Mia's dedicated to this dig. And so is Rik. He's been absolutely marvellous all the time Dad was ill. And I don't really want to sit here and listen to your accusations."

Pippa was surprised at the vehemence of her words. Here she was defending Rik and Mia when what Mike said might be really true. But she trusted her father's judgement. He had said he couldn't do without Fenton, and Mike was displaying the classic symptoms of jealousy.

"Suit yourself, Pippa," he said, "but I assure you I would never have said anything if I hadn't been very worried. Besides, do you think that Fenton would really stay on here indefinitely with his qualifications? Unless, of course, *he was in charge.*"

"Really, Mike," she said, "I don't want to hear this." She began to get up but he put his hand out to detain her.

"I think you should. This is an extremely prestigious dig and Fenton is very ambitious."

She pulled away from him, looking at him with angry eyes. There was no way Pippa was going to sit and listen to this.

"So, Fenton's got to you, too, has he, Pippa?" Mike's expression was ugly.

"What do you mean?"

"You're very much like your father. And in his eyes Fenton can do no wrong. He seems to have managed to fool you, too."

Pippa reacted angrily. She wasn't going to be spoken to like that. "Look, Mike, you've made it quite clear what you think about Rik. But I suggest you leave me out of it. I don't know what's going on here - and I don't really want to. I just want Dad to get well."

"So you don't care about what happened in the accident? To get to the truth."

It was an inexcusable thing to say. Pippa swallowed.

93

In the past they had been close, but it gave him no right to speak to her like that.

"I think," she said, "that the best thing for you to do, Mike, is to discuss this with my father when he feels better. I don't want to be caught up in this. And I care for him, you know that. What right have you to say otherwise?"

Her voice was raised; she could see Rik looking across at them. "Rik may be ambitious, even arrogant, but I don't think he'd hurt Dad."

"Wouldn't he?" Mike persisted.

"I know you're under pressure," she said, "but, please, don't take it out on me."

Rik and Mia were rolling up the maps and preparing to come over. Mike was still looking at them. "Can't you see they have everything under control? Just as it suits them. How do you know what's going on, Pippa? I just want you to think about what I've said."

He pulled off his sunglasses and wiped his face. "Right, I'm going to get on with shoring up that tunnel. Come over later if you want to have a look," he said, then he strode off towards the excavations.

Pippa knew why he made the move. Rik and Mia were walking towards them.

"What did he want?" Rik asked.

For a moment Pippa thought she could recognise anxiety in his voice. Could any of it be true? She dismissed the thought. It was preposterous to think that either Rik or Mia could be involved in her father's accident.

Anyway, Rik had been down below her. She didn't even want to acknowledge the fact she'd had that thought. She knew he was ambitious and arrogant, but that was all he was. Pippa had seen nothing to suggest that he was capable of inflicting harm on anyone just to further his career. Her father relied on him completely.

Mia had been so cut up about the accident. Pippa remembered the tears in her eyes, and how she had sat with Pippa, who'd been so glad of Mia's calm manner and support. She had never thought Mike was vicious - but she'd evidently been wrong about a lot of things regarding him. Should she tell Rik and Mia about his accusations?

"What did he want?" Rik repeated.

"Not a lot," she lied. "He was asking me to go over and have a look at the tunnel."

"I'd keep away if I were you," Rik said. "You're doing a good job here." He looked at the tray of broken pottery, which had been dug up from the tomb. Pippa had sorted through and labelled it carefully.

"Big deal." She smiled. "Thanks anyway."

"It's always the little things that count, in archaeology I mean," Mia said. "I'm afraid Mike sometimes doesn't seem to understand that." Her face was serious. She turned. "Still, I have to get on."

"So do I," Rik said. "I'll get the boys to brew up. We'll have some tea before you go back to the hospital." He grinned.

The two of them left Pippa playing her pottery jigsaw game with deft and skilful fingers.

She looked up from the task a few minutes later to see Ahmed gesticulating. She had left him severely alone since the police visited the hotel. It had been quite awkward but Rik had assured her that he'd had a good telling off. Now he was beckoning to her, his thin arm waving lazily in the stiflingly-hot late afternoon. She glanced at her cup. Empty. She felt parched constantly.

And Ahmed was still beckoning her. Perhaps Mike really needed her?

But Rik had warned her not to go and investigate the tunnel. Pippa told herself she wouldn't go very near anyway. It wouldn't hurt just to look at what Mike wanted. He was definitely calling to her. Perhaps the boys had found something interesting?

Closing the book in which she'd been writing the details of the pottery, she stood up, dusted herself down, adjusted her hat and glasses and made her way over to where Mike and the boys were working to shore up the tunnel, which had collapsed burying so many weeks of hard work.

Ahmed had disappeared, hidden, she supposed, by the great mounds of sand and wooden stakes which lay at the ready. She could see the long white robes and turbans of the other boys as they sweated over the labour of getting the tunnel entrance free again. To an amateur, the dig looked like a massive, untidy, building site.

Then she could see Ahmed again, standing on a huge mound, looking for all the world as nimble as a monkey. He was pointing behind him excitedly up towards the rock wall which, after years of excavations, appeared to be a network of rough steps and stairways and ledges.

Pippa couldn't see a thing, but her curiosity was increasing as she got nearer.

"Ahmed," she called, "what do you want?" Perhaps he wasn't even signing to her? She couldn't understand it. Why would he call her anyway after what had happened? There was no doubt that he'd got into very hot water after the police incident.

She was walking in the direction of where she thought the entrance to the tomb had been. Again, Ahmed disappeared. He was probably with Mike, the two of them hidden by the other workers. She hesitated, looked round and saw Rik Fenton directing another group of native workmen, the maps rolled up under his arm.

He lifted his head and seeing her, cupped his hands to his mouth and shouted, "Where are you going?"

"Over here, to Mike."

She shouted as hard as she could, but he probably couldn't hear because of the wind. However, the strong breeze, filled with sand, carried the thin, piping voice of Ahmed right into her ears.

"Missy, over here." The sound seemed to come from behind a pile of thin logs, resembling bundles of firewood, which were stacked neatly against the rock wall about fifty metres up.

Pippa squinted into the sun and began to walk carefully round to where the tomb's entrance had been. She was close to the rock wall but couldn't see Ahmed any more. She stopped hesitantly.

"Mike," she called, "do you want me?"

There was no reply but the wind. She looked round. Most of the boys were digging about fifty metres away but, again, there was no Ahmed. She felt very annoyed. He must be playing her up. Hadn't he any work to do? Her face was burning with heat and the exertion and she was just about to turn back when she heard a strident shout.

"Run, Pippa, quick!"

She obeyed instantly and, only a second later, heard the massive thud as the rough and splintered wooden beams came crashing down behind her. She put her hands up to her mouth and screamed. They had smashed on the very spot she'd been standing. If she hadn't moved, she'd have been dead.

She knew who'd shouted. It was Rik. He called out as he ran madly over, trying to calm her.

"Didn't I tell you to keep away from the tomb entrance?" he demanded as he reached the spot. There was no malice in his tone, just concern.

And Pippa was terrified.

She felt as if all the breath had been knocked out of her body. She sat down on a heap of sand dizzily and he pushed her head between her knees. She stayed like that for a few moments then she put up her hand and clung to his strong fingers, interlacing them with her own.

"Better now?" he said after a few moments.

"I really thought I was going to faint," she answered shamefacedly.

"I would have, too, if that lot had fallen off near me," he said. There was the faintest flicker of a smile, but it didn't reach his eyes. He looked very grim. "Anyway, what were you doing?"

"I was following Ahmed. He kept beckoning to me, calling me towards the tomb. I thought Mike wanted me."

She had never heard Rik Fenton swear before, but he did now, loudly and at length.

"You don't think it was *on purpose*?" she asked.

"Listen, Pippa, a lot of strange things are happening round here. And they have to stop." He picked up her hat which had fallen off and handed it to her. "You look very white."

He took her hand. "Come on," he said, "let's get a cup of tea inside you, and then we'll talk - decide what to do. I don't want you here at the site any more."

"You don't want me here any more?" she repeated as he helped her over the debris and stones back towards the tents.

"It's not a question of that, Pippa," he said. "I'm afraid you're in danger. And that was just a taste of it."

"Then you think it *was* on purpose?"

"At the moment I don't know what to think," he said, "but I don't like it. Neither can I risk it. It's enough having the professor in hospital, never mind you as well."

"Hi, Pippa, what happened?" They heard Mike's voice and his feet running up behind them. Rik Fenton stopped and waited for the other man to catch up with them.

"You didn't see then?" he asked. Mike shook his head.

"No. Ahmed just told me. Are you all right?"

Pippa stood between the two men, who were staring at each other in a hostile manner.

"Yes, I am all right, thanks to Rik," she said. "If he hadn't shouted, I'd probably be dead."

"I told the boys to make that wood safe," Mike said, "and someone's going to pay for this."

"Yes, they are," Rik's tone was hard.

"Well, I'm fine," Pippa said, although she didn't feel it. Her legs were decidedly shaky. Suddenly, Rik put his arms about her shoulders. They were facing Mike.

"I'm taking Pippa for a cup of tea," he said. "And afterwards, I'd like a word with you - if you have the time. Come on, Pippa."

"Oh, I'll find the time," Mike said, as the two of them walked away.

Inside, all Pippa could think about, was that Mike had not shown any kind of concern about the accident. He was behaving as if she were a complete stranger.

* * *

CHAPTER 9

"Do you think Ahmed pushed those logs down?" she asked Rik as she sipped her tea. "Why would he do it? I don't understand what's going on? Who would do something like that?"

Rik Fenton shook his head. She couldn't read his expression and she had an uncanny feeling that he was holding something back from her.

Just what was going on at this site? Ever since she'd arrived things felt wrong. Pippa had always prided herself on her intuition, and her thoughts ran back to her first hour in Egypt, when neither her father nor Mike had come to collect her from the airport. Instead, Rik Fenton had been sent to meet her.

Afterwards, she'd had to face the fact that things had changed between her and Mike and it was none of her fault. Mike had changed, but why? She remembered his hostility towards Mia Gabal and both Rik's and Mia's evident intention not to leave Pippa alone. Then there was her father's accident and her own narrow escape.

She felt drained. As she looked at the handsome, dark face of the man her father said he couldn't do without, she wondered at her own feelings for him and wished she knew exactly what his relationship with Mia Gabal was.

"Please, Rik, I just want to know what's going on. And I certainly don't want something like this happening again."

He stretched his hand up to the tent flaps, then brought it down closing them. "I'm sorry, Pippa, but I can't explain any of the things that have happened or that are happening now. You'll just have to trust me."

"You mean you could explain them if you wanted to?"

"I'm not even sure of that," he said quietly. "But there is one thing I do know. You should go back to Cairo and stay in the hotel. Just keep close to your father and leave Mia and me to look after things here."

So they were back to square one again; Rik and Mia in charge. And Mike had warned her that was what they wanted. She felt utterly confused.

"But why can't I be here?" she persisted.

"I think you know the answer to that," he said, "but, if you can't trust me, there's nothing I can do. I'm unable to say anything to you but, hopefully, things will be resolved soon."

It seemed such a patronising thing to say. He must have been reading her thoughts. "I realise that sounds pompous but, really, Pippa, it's all I can say."

"I know it's something connected with Mike," she said suddenly. She saw the wariness in his expression now; and she recognised she was getting warm.

"I want to think it's just because you two don't get on," she added, "but I know it isn't that either. It's all beyond me - but, yes, I will go back to Cairo if it's only for a few days. Some holiday this has turned out to be." She knew the remark sounded like the kind of thing a peeved teenager would say, and she was sorry. He was smiling and she thought it was because he'd got what he wanted.

"That's absolutely great," he said. "And, Pippa, I

101

promise you, when your father gets better and things are sorted out, Egypt and I will give you the best holiday you've ever had."

"Promises, promises," she said, but she didn't feel like joking. She'd play along with them a little more, but Pippa was determined to find out what was the mystery.

* * *

Pippa read up quite a lot about the area when she was staying at the Hotel Saladin. Her father had moved into the suite with her after he was discharged and they seemed to be getting on very well. It was almost like old times. And it suited them to be so near the hospital in case he had a relapse.

She also toured around and saw a lot of Cairo. Her father was on the mend now, but he still never mentioned the troubled site and she didn't want to pressurise him. But she was no nearer the truth. She behaved like the perfect tourist yet, all the time, she couldn't get the problems of the site out of her head.

Her father was in no condition to discuss what happened, and she knew she'd get nothing out of Rik Fenton. She'd tried talking to Mia Gabal, but the Egyptian doctor was just as secretive.

Mike's involvement with the project confused her, too. For instance, why had he left that excellent job in the South American university to come back and work with her father in Egypt?

He wasn't like Rik - he didn't have to establish himself. But, there he was in Egypt, working for a great deal less than he'd been paid before. If he didn't like the Cairo site, why did he stay? He'd talked incessantly of South America when he was in London. Then he'd told her his main ambition was to return. The more she thought about it all, the more puzzled she became.

Pippa sighed and paused, putting down her pen. The telephone was ringing. She felt listless and lazy. The heat was getting to her. She could recognise the signs. And she'd been thinking of England. She hadn't realised how much she missed it, since all the unpleasant things had happened.

"All right, I'm coming," she said, forcing herself to hurry. She picked up the receiver and was very surprised.

"Pippa? How are you?" It was Mike. "Pippa, I'd like to see you. Soon."

"Would you?" she asked. "When?" The surprise was turning to suspicion.

"Tonight." His tone was urgent.

"All right, where?"

"Why not on the site?"

Pippa's heart gave a jump. Why didn't he come into Cairo? Why did he want her out there? With all the things that had been happening, she couldn't help feeling suspicious.

Just then she heard a step behind her. She turned swiftly to see Mia Gabal coming in through the huge patio windows, from where she'd been sitting with Professor Adams by the side of the pool.

She had driven over, leaving Rik to get on with the work. In fact, Pippa thought, Mia had been spending a lot of time with her father lately and it seemed to have helped. The professor was enjoying her calm but cheerful company.

When Mia saw Pippa on the phone she nodded and putting up her hand, moved backwards. Pippa mouthed to her, "It's Mike," and the doctor withdrew tact-fully.

"All right, Mike, I'll meet you tonight. It sounds urgent. Is it?"

"It's about Fenton."

"Rik? What's happened?"

"I don't want to talk about it on the telephone," was his reply. "And I advise you not to say anything to your father."

"If that's the way you want it," she said. "Right, I'll look forward to it."

"Oh, I'll send Ahmed to fetch you," Mike said. She felt a tiny shiver at the words. "Then I can bring you back. And, after, perhaps we could have dinner?" It all seemed innocent enough, but quite out of character. And why shouldn't she tell her father?

She worried then, anxious about the conversation, what she was going to hear about Rik, and especially about being fetched by Ahmed. But, somehow, she had to get to the bottom of the whole thing. She would take the risk, if there was a risk, just to find out. She wouldn't tell her father, but she was going to tell Mia.

Mia looked at her seriously. "So Mike wants to meet you on the site tonight?"

"Yes, then he's bringing me back to Cairo and we're going out for a meal."

"Why do you think he wants to see you?" Mia asked.

"I don't know," Pippa said honestly. "But, as you probably know, Mike once meant something to me. It hardly seems like it now after all the problems but, in London, I thought . . ."

"Yes?" Mia prompted.

"Well, what I mean is, that when he came back from

South America, he was a different man. And I thought it was all going to be the same out here."

"I don't think things ever stay the same," Mia said. "Take Rik, for instance."

When she spoke his name she pronounced it very softly. Pippa could feel the little pang again. The two of them were so close. And why shouldn't they be? They spent the whole of their working lives together. She was thinking of that intimate moment in her unconscious father's room.

"You like Rik, don't you?" Mia asked.

Pippa nodded. "I don't always understand him though," she admitted.

"Neither do I," Mia Gabal said ruefully, "but I assure you, Pippa, that he is utterly trustworthy."

"Why do you say that?" Pippa asked.

"I just thought you might need to hear it. Now I must go over to your father. He's looking bored and I think it's time I told him about that wooden figure we discovered on the fourth level yesterday. That should cheer him up."

"Yes, you have found some beautiful things inside the tomb, Mia," Pippa said admiringly. "You must be very proud of such a heritage."

"We always have been," the doctor said quietly as she got up to leave, "but we didn't like sharing them with everyone."

"You mean you didn't like foreign archaeologists digging them up and running off with them?"

"Hardly running off with them now," Mia joked. "But, as for the Victorians - well, that was different."

"Mia?" The professor called to her.

"Oh, excuse me," she smiled. "I'd better go to him. And,

Pippa, don't worry, I'm sure everything will be all right."

She was walking swiftly across to the pool. Pippa watched her squatting beside her father's garden chair, showing him some photographs.

What did she mean when she said everything would be all right? It was all so frustrating. Everyone seemed to know what was going on except Pippa herself.

A few minutes later, Pippa came out of the bedroom to find Mia by the telephone. "Oh, by the way, Pippa, I forgot. I'll take you out to the site tonight. I need to go over and see Rik anyway. I'll give him a bell and he'll tell Mike."

"Thank you, Mia. That'll be great," replied Pippa, relieved she didn't need to rely on Ahmed.

* * *

Mia was in a quiet mood on the journey and Pippa decided it wouldn't be a good idea to ask the older woman many questions. In any case, if she did, it would look as if she didn't trust Rik. She was sure that whatever Mia knew, she would never be disloyal to him. Once, it was on the tip of Pippa's tongue to ask Mia how long she and Rik had been going out, but she couldn't bring herself to. Instead, they chatted about things like if Pippa enjoyed her job and when she planned to return to London. Mia also seemed very interested in Mike's South American trip.

"I don't really know a lot about it, Mia," Pippa said, "except whatever happened there hooked Mike. He can't wait to get back. But I've no idea why he left if he liked it so much."

"Strange indeed," said Mia.

Her eyes were intent on the traffic conditions. She

was careful at the wheel, and Pippa was grateful for it. She was getting used to travelling to the site, but not to the irresponsible drivers on the way.

"I'm extremely interested myself in the South American scene," Mia added. "I've heard that some of the native excavations are entirely fascinating. Indeed, I hear they are almost as interesting as ours. Do you have any first-hand information about the dig Mike was working on. I'd like to contact the professor on the project."

"I'm afraid I know hardly anything," confessed Pippa. "He used to write and tell me what the country itself was like, but that's all."

"Used to?"

"Yes. He stopped writing after a while. Pressure of work, I expect."

"Doubtless," said Mia. "I know all about that."

It was such a beautiful evening they didn't talk much after. Both seemed lost in their own thoughts. As Mia dropped Pippa off outside Mike's tent, she said, "Have a great time, Pippa. I'll see you tomorrow. *And don't worry.*" With that, she drove off across the site, leaving Pippa to wonder if she'd given the impression she'd been more than usually anxious.

The first thing Pippa noticed about Mike was that he'd made an effort to dress up. He was wearing a cream, linen suit. She was extremely surprised, and even more so when she saw the two canvas bags placed by the head of the camp bed. But his face was white and drawn. He was evidently under more strain than ever.

"Are you leaving us?" she said, sitting down at the table and looking at the bags. If only she could get near to Mike again. If only to get him to tell her what was wrong.

"Yes." He was having difficulty looking her in the eyes. She couldn't understand why he was so nervous with her. "That's why I wanted to talk to you on your own. You see, Pippa, although things haven't been right between us, there have been reasons."

"Reasons?" she repeated, wondering if she was going to get to the bottom of the mystery at last. "Go on then." She wasn't sure how she felt about his decision. How could he just go? The project was nowhere near finished. What about his contract, for instance? There had to be an excellent reason for Mike Nash abandoning her father.

"Well," he said, "I'm getting out. I've had enough."

"Enough of what?"

"Of everything."

"What's Dad going to think of this, Mike? After all he's done for you. What's gone wrong? You left South America just to be with him. What's changed?"

She was watching him closely now. An expression came to his face that she'd seen before; only, then, it had been one of her patients, a depressed man, who was near to despair. She felt extremely worried.

"I have nothing against your father, Pippa," Mike retorted. "But I can't be here any longer. And it's Fenton's fault. And Mia Gabal's."

She couldn't be sorry for him if it was only that. How could he allow his jealousy for them jeopardise his whole career? It was petty.

"If they hadn't interfered in my life, I would have stayed," he continued. "But I just can't work with them any more and, as your father takes notice only of them, he's not interested in me. I'll find something else. In fact, I have plans. And Egypt doesn't come into them."

"Well, I suppose that's something," Pippa said. "Are you off to South America again? You enjoyed it over there, didn't you?"

"Enjoyed?" His eyes seemed unnaturally bright and his voice hoarse. She could see he was in a state of nervous tension. "I don't think *enjoyed* is quite the word I'd use, my dear."

"Well, whatever?" She shrugged, looking away. She hardly knew what to say to him any more.

"I want you to be very careful, Pippa."

"What do you mean?" The next sentence amazed her.

"Someone . . ." he paused, moistening his lips with his tongue, ". . . someone might try to hurt you."

She stared at him, determined not to show her own nervousness.

"Hurt me? How? You don't mean Ahmed, by any chance?" She attempted a smile.

"Perhaps. I don't know, but I won't be here any more to protect you, and then who knows what could happen? It's no joke, Pippa. Egypt's a dangerous place." The way he said it scared her slightly. As if he was threatening her. But Pippa was used to people saying the wildest things. She kept her cool.

"I don't understand what you're trying to tell me, Mike," she replied. "Can't you just come out and say what you really mean?"

"I'm trying to tell you that you'd be better off in London. You'd be safer. And I can't say anything else." He sounded like he meant it. There was a high, almost hysterical tone in his voice.

"In other words, you think I shouldn't be here? That I'd be safer elsewhere? I suppose it was because of that silly sarcophagus? Surely you're not superstitious, Mike? You're a scientist." Pippa knew he didn't mean *that* but, all the time, she was trying to draw him out further.

He didn't answer, only breathed in deeply. So she tried another way. "And, as for *protecting* me, I don't think that's likely any more, is it, Mike? It was you who changed things between us. Remember?"

"I know."

She was amazed at the admission. "And is there a reason for that too?"

"Isn't there always?" he replied. "We were probably just wrong for each other. Nothing stays the same. Except all this." He gestured hopelessly. "And that brings me to the second reason for me leaving. If, after I've gone, you hear things about me, ignore them and, remember, Pippa, *none of it was my fault.*" He was holding her arm now, his eyes filled with a look of sheer desperation.

"None of what? What is it that everyone else seems to know about but no-one will explain?" She hadn't meant to blurt it out like that, but she was exasperated.

"I can't explain. I told you that. But if you're not careful, you might find out too much." It was quite annoying, given that he'd invited her out to the site to tell her something and the conversation had ended with nothing but riddles.

"I can tell *you* something, Mike," she replied coolly. "I don't know what's going on here, but I do intend to find out what *you're* mixed up in. Evidently, it seems to be dangerous, as you all . . ."

"All?" He looked startled.

"As you all keep telling me to be careful," she repeated. "I will be, I promise you, but I'll still find out - and so will my father. I shall ask him what's going on here first, and then, if I have to, I shall speak to the police. Maybe they'll be able to put in the missing pieces." It was a complete

110

bluff, but Pippa could be devious when she wanted to be.

"I don't think that would be a very good idea," he said, more calmly. "They're always getting the wrong end of the stick."

"We'll see," she said. "But, there is one thing - and remember I speak from experience - each one of us is responsible for our own actions and has to face it in the end. So, whatever has been happening here, it's no good shifting the blame on other shoulders." Anger stained Pippa's cheeks red as she continued, "Now I think I want to get back to Cairo, Mike. This trip to see you has been an utter waste of time. I would rather have stayed with Dad. Perhaps when we drive back you might add something to the mystery you're making of everything."

She stood up suddenly. "Are you nearly ready? You seem to be travelling extra light. But it's not my business, is it?" She looked round at the pathetic amount of luggage. "And, Mike, even though things haven't worked out between us, I suppose I'm sorry. We did have some good times in the past."

"We did," he agreed. "Right, you go on out to the jeep and I'll follow in a minute. I'm leaving it in Cairo to be picked up from the airport tomorrow. I've still a few small things to collect."

"And you're not saying goodbye to anyone - not even your precious Ahmed? Do you take me for a fool, Mike?" She said it in purpose to goad him; to make him tell her the truth. And her idea appeared to have the desired effect because Mike swung round again to face her.

Pippa was quite fed up with the whole thing - everyone was treating her like a complete idiot. There was no way Mike nor even Rik was getting away with it any longer. If something was about to happen to her or her father, she intended to know about it first.

"Well, is it Ahmed I have to watch. Or someone else?" she queried.

"Certainly not Ahmed," he said, and his voice was toneless. "And that was quite uncalled for. Now, please go outside, Pippa, and leave me alone for a minute."

Mike wouldn't be drawn either. Everyone intended to *warn* her about some mythical thing that might or might not happen, but to *tell* her absolutely nothing. She'd had enough.

Pippa shrugged angrily and quickly stepped outside his tent into the dark. Perhaps the cold air of the desert night might help dispel the way she was feeling inside. Hurt. And very annoyed indeed. She looked up at the wonderful array of stars and swore.

* * *

CHAPTER 10

No one heard her though. There was no sign of anyone, just the dim lights which were the workers' tents and the excavations looming black and eerie in the distance. Somewhere she could hear voices but these were quite incoherent.

Pippa could see the jeep and, slowly, began to walk towards it. Still, she moved warily, conscious of all the warnings she had been given and, especially, Mike's. Then she gasped. There *was* someone else wandering around in the dark.

Pippa knew who it was instinctively. There was no mistaking the dark figure jumping nimbly out of the back of the stationary vehicle. She would have recognised Ahmed anywhere, even if the moonlight had not betrayed the little Egyptian.

Suddenly, she had a feeling he wanted her to notice him; to see what he was doing, just like he tricked her when the logs fell. She was going to be more careful this time and felt sure he was certainly up to no good. Ahmed was standing very still, looking in her direction, the white of his robes glinting brightly in the moonlight.

Pippa regarded him warily, sizing up the situation. She remembered what had happened the last time she followed him. He probably still had it in for her. And all because she'd touched the great sarcophagus in the pyramid. Could it be possible? It didn't make sense - but, then, what did in Egypt?

She waited uncertainly, hoping he'd move away, She was finding it quite unnerving having someone stand staring at her like that in the dark.

She looked away from Ahmed towards Rik's tent. He hadn't even emerged when Mia had dropped her off. What was he doing? He wouldn't be near enough to save her this time if anything went wrong. She swallowed, uncertainly, biting her bottom lip.

Then two enormous shadows were thrown across the canvas of Rik's tent. He and Mia were probably together again. The doctor had left her vehicle outside anyway. Of course, they wanted to be with each other all the time.

That was probably why Mia had been so enthusiastic in offering Pippa a lift. She couldn't keep away from him. She'd said she needed to see him. It couldn't possibly be business every moment of their time together. And, probably, that was why Rik had told Pippa earlier it would be better if she'd stayed in Cairo.

Pippa shook her head. Well, they were going to get what they wanted. She'd said she would go back to Cairo with Mike - and after that what? The decision came swiftly as she watched those moving shadows in the tent.

She might as well go back to England. She'd lost Mike; her father didn't need her any more and there was nothing she could do about Rik and Mia, even if what Mike said about them was true. She'd had enough of it all. Egypt was no place for her any longer.

As for Rik Fenton - she didn't know how to analyse her

feelings regarding him. When she'd managed to get near to him she'd found him surprisingly attractive. But what of it? He belonged to someone else. Besides, his work was the most important thing to him.

Pippa felt her exasperation returning, and shrugged it off again. There was little point in pursuing that line of thought.

She glanced back to where Ahmed had been standing. He'd evidently tired of waiting for her. She turned towards Mike's tent and, at the same moment, he extinguished the gas lantern. He must be ready.

She decided she would write a note to Mia and Rik when she got back to the hotel explaining her decision for leaving so suddenly. Then she wouldn't have to face Rik again. He wouldn't mind really. Of course, she would have to think of a good excuse for her father. But he'd understand she had to return to work sometime.

Her thoughts were making Pippa feel extremely miserable and confused. Trying to clear her head, she walked purposefully towards the vehicle that Mike and Rik used jointly. She was thinking about the day she and Rik Fenton had gone to see the Pyramids. Had it only been a couple of weeks ago? It seemed like a thousand years.

Anyway, she was confident she'd be able to explain how she felt to her father. After all the friction she'd experienced, she could understand now why he looked so tired but, in her heart, she still couldn't believe that Mia and Rik wanted to get rid of him.

Rik owed him too much, and Mia seemed extremely fond of him. Neither of them seemed to be acting a part. Pippa would just have to talk to her father about Mike's accusation. She owed it him, just in case. At least she could trust *him*. But she was afraid to upset him after his illness.

Why Mike had asked her over to the site tonight especially was still a mystery to her, but she expected she'd find out the answer to it all in the end. It couldn't be just because he was leaving the dig.

She was very near the jeep now and there was no sign of Ahmed again. He'd evidently had his fun trying to frighten her. She hesitated, then looked round. Her heart nearly jumped out of her chest. There he was, watching her once more, only about ten metres away, leaning silently against the guy rope of one of the workers' tents.

She breathed in deeply, looking behind her. Mike must be on his way. What could hurt her here? The sudden thought returned, that this time Rik Fenton wasn't around to help. She shook it off. Why did she think she needed him anyway?

"I don't need anyone," she said to herself determinedly as she reached the side of the jeep. The vehicle's tall bulk threw an enormous shadow across the sand. Why had Ahmed been messing about in the jeep? What could he have been doing in there? She had to find out.

She walked round to the back. At first, all she could see were empty seats but, then, something caught her eye, glinting brightly in the moonlight. Whatever it was, was positioned under one of the seats. Pippa could see the sacking, which had covered it, had been pushed aside.

Catching hold of the grab handles, she pulled herself up inside the vehicle and squatted to look. She gasped. What the moonlight revealed was certainly eye-catching - a crate, wide open and crammed with archaeological objects. She even recognised some she'd entered and labelled herself.

What were these precious things doing stowed away under the seat of the jeep? Where were they going? Who had put them there? Was this what Ahmed had been doing?

She stretched out her hand and picked up a small, wooden figure holding a crude musical instrument. What would something as unusual as this fetch on the foreign black market?

A horrible, cold feeling was running through her. Why were treasures from the tomb being stowed away in the vehicle? There was no way that rings, bracelets, amulets and statues from the Eleventh Dynasty would be jumbled up like this. No way at all.

Pippa put down the small statue and pulled the crate shut. She was afraid and sick all at the same time. The treasures were being stolen - there was no doubt about that - but who was responsible. It couldn't be Ahmed. Hadn't he led her to them? That meant he had a grudge against someone else. Someone who had crossed him.

The thought struck her like an arrow head. Who else? Who had given him the sharp end of his tongue? Who had saved her from the falling logs? Who was the jeep's usual driver? She couldn't bear the thought that Rik Fenton was a cheat and a thief.

She got up from her knees and wiped her hands down the side of her legs as if trying to clean off some awful disease. Then she pushed back her heavy hair. It seemed to fall like a lead weight on her shoulders. Her father had trusted Rik. How could he? And Mia as well. She was an Egyptian; these articles were her heritage. But who else could it be? It just couldn't be them.

"Don't go jumping to conclusions," she told herself, trying to calm her wild imaginings.

She was just jumping out when a hand on her shoulder made her heart lurch like a crazy frog.

"What are you doing?" Mike asked, his face dark and sullen in the moonlight. "Why didn't you get in the front?"

"I . . . I . . ." she faltered, trying to pull her thoughts together.

"What's the matter?" His voice was cold and unfeeling, like a stranger's.

"Nothing. I was looking for . . . my hair slide. I lost it when Rik and I went to the Pyramids. . ."

"You were looking for your hair slide in the dark?"

"Yes." It was a stupid explanation but it gave her the time she needed to compose herself.

"No, Pippa," he said. He was holding her by the shoulders, towering over her. "There's something else, isn't there? You were looking at something else."

"Yes," she admitted. "Let go of me, please. You're hurting."

"Oh, I'm sorry," he said and his voice seemed softer. "But I think *I* know what you saw."

"What?" She stared at him, playing for time, trying to work out what was happening.

If Mike knew about the things, Rik couldn't have put them there. Her heartbeat increased.

"Let's continue this conversation in the front." He threw his luggage in the back of the jeep.

"No," she said, suddenly wary. "I'd rather stay here."

"You won't when you know what I'm going to say," he said, leading her round to the passenger seat and opening the door.

"Please, Mike, I don't know if I want to go with you." Suddenly, he was close to her and his face was drawn. "Unless, of course, you can provide an explanation," she added.

"I'll tell you, Pippa," he said, "but I don't think you're going to like it. In fact, you may not even believe it."

"Try me," she said, still unwilling to get up into the vehicle.

"I think you should get in first," he replied. She was going to have to comply; otherwise she'd never find out.

"All right." Pippa gave in and then he stood beside her, blocking the passenger seat door.

"You saw the finds?" His tone was flat; his face openly serious.

She nodded, looking him straight in the eyes. "What are you doing with them, Mike? *You* put them there, didn't you?

"Yes." He closed the door of the vehicle and she saw him walk round the front. She followed him with her eyes. He had admitted it. Why?

He swung himself up into the seat and started the engine. As it sprang into life, he turned to speak to her. "Yes," he repeated, "I'm *saving* them." He pushed the automatic gear into place and the jeep jerked forward.

"Saving them?"

"Yes."

The answer was so calm that she thought Mike couldn't have noticed the incredulity in her question. The sand dunes were sliding fast below them as the jeep gathered speed. It seemed that Mike was in a big hurry.

"Who from, Mike? Who wants our treasures?"

He turned from the wheel. "I said you weren't going to like it. I'm taking the artefacts from the tomb to Cairo. They need protection from Rik and Mia."

"Rik? Mia?" Her heart was thumping. He must be lying. Yet a few minutes before, even she had considered that possibility. She cleared her throat but her voice was unnaturally high. "Do you know what you're saying?"

"I know very well." His voice was free of any emotion.

"Are you saying that Rik and Mia were going to steal them?"

"Yes," he answered tersely. "That's exactly what I'm saying."

"I can't believe it," she said. Rik might be arrogant and high-handed, but he wasn't a crook; she was sure of that.

"I said you wouldn't believe it. You don't want to believe it. That's what you mean, isn't it, Pippa?"

"No."

"You're besotted with the man, aren't you?"

"No, I'm not."

"That's why you won't believe what's under your nose."

"How can you say that?" she protested, but even to her own ears her words sounded half-hearted.

"It shows, Pippa. You're in love with him."

She hated the way he said it. As though he was jealous. As though there was anything between her and Mike still. And, if there had been, there was nothing to be jealous about anyway. It was true she was attracted to Rik, but she couldn't be in love with him. He was in love with Mia.

"You're being ridiculous. And, even if I was, it wouldn't blind me to his faults. Besides, what good would it do Rik or Mia to sabotage the dig? They're both crazy about Dad."

"You're a psychologist. What do you think?" He scoffed. "What about your father falling? What about the logs? Who was on the scene straight away? It wasn't me, was it? No, it was your precious Rik."

"Shut up, Mike," she said, wishing she had never agreed to go back to Cairo with him. She felt she almost hated

120

him and his wild, malicious accusations. She leaned back in her seat, trying to think rationally.

Eventually, she said, "Why don't you say what you really mean, Mike? I know you hate Rik, but as for calling him a crook, I can't believe you'd be as jealous of him as that."

"Jealous?" He spat out the word. "Of him? Oh, no, I wouldn't have his life for anything."

"I'm sorry for you, Mike," Pippa said, staring straight ahead. "What happened? You were so dedicated, enthusiastic, a wonderful archaeologist..." She stopped. The look on his face was awful, even frightening. She'd experienced looks like that before in her work; both vulnerable and crazy people exposed to emotions they couldn't cope with. It drove them wild. Psychotics. But to see that on the face of someone she had once cared about personally, saddened her beyond belief.

"I can't let him go on like this," he spat. "Fenton's selling them off so he can finance those pet schemes of his, like going to heaven-knows-where and making a glorious name for himself. One or two of them would give him enough money to do what he wants for life. Some private collectors would pay a fortune for stuff like that."

"That's a terrible thing to say, Mike. I can't believe I'm hearing it." She was determined now it wasn't true. "And, come on, how could Mia be in on it? She's Egyptian. She wouldn't let those things out of the country."

"You're so naive, Pippa. Like a child," Mike said nastily. His voice was cold and clipped, and she wondered how she'd ever been stupid enough to think a man like Mike was for her.

"Gabal's in on this up to her eye-balls," he continued.

"She's playing along with Rik so she can nab him and carve up the dig at the same time. Do you think Egyptians want foreign archaeologists raping their land? She can't stand your father. She's only there on site to watch and sift everything with a fine-tooth comb and then report back to the authorities. She'd do anything she could to get this dig closed up."

It was a plausible theory, but Pippa couldn't believe it. She sat, in silence, as Mike drove madly on, looking out into the black night, trying to make some sense out of anything he'd told her, but it just didn't seem to add up.

"And what about Ahmed? Where does he fit in? I saw him just before you came out and he was definitely trying to catch my attention. In fact I think he *wanted* me to find the treasures."

"Ah, Ahmed is priceless." Mike was laughing excitably. "You got off on the wrong foot with him properly. You hit on exactly the right thing to upset him. To his mind, the tomb treasures are sacred, and anyone who takes them will be regarded as a grave robber, liable to be dealt with by the sand-devil."

"Stop it," Pippa cried furiously. "It's just a lot of superstitious clap-trap, and you know it, Mike."

"Ahmed doesn't have to get his own back," Mike persisted, "because he expects *retribution* to do it for him." He lifted his eyebrows at her. Then, turning back to his driving, began laughing out loud. There was no doubt about it. Mike was unbalanced.

"I'd like to get out," Pippa said, pressing her face to the glass window. "Now."

"Are you crazy?" Mike shouted as she caught hold of the door handle. "You're on a road in the middle of the desert." His mood was changing. She was frightened but she wasn't going to show it. She'd used the *getting out* technique to shock him. He caught her arm, "Look, I'm sorry if I scared you but . . ."

"You didn't scare me," Pippa interrupted. "I'm just sick of your company and your silly accusations. Take me back to my father, please. I don't want to be near you for a moment longer than necessary."

That shut him up.

* * *

While Mike drove on in silence, Pippa considered everything that he'd said. Who was behind Ahmed? She didn't believe it was any superstitious fear. Maybe it was Mike himself. But what was his motive? Surely it had to be more than jealousy? Something had tipped him over the edge. Did he need the cash? He'd never complained about being hard-up; he'd always lived well- at least, when she knew him. But that had been a different Mike. She didn't know this one and she didn't want to.

"Where did you say you were going, Mike?" she asked. She had to be one step ahead.

"Cairo."

"No, I mean after that. Where will you find work?"

"Abroad," he replied tersely, his narrowed eyes never leaving the road.

That was the only reply she was going to get. At least, he appeared to have his feelings under control. She didn't speak again until they were crossing the Nile Bridge. She felt safer now she was in the city. She decided to try again.

"Mike," she probed, "are you sure it wasn't *you* who

loaded those things in the crate first? I know you use the vehicle as well as Rik."

"So now you're accusing me," he said. "Well, I credited you with more sense than to try that. It's such a pity."

"Why?"

"Because you'll just have to stay with me now until the whole thing is sorted." His voice was hard and flat and directed as if to a stranger. "I can't have you blurting out to the police the kind of accusation you've just made."

"Who mentioned the police?"

"I did. And there's no chance of involving them, Pippa. I'll get Rik Fenton in my own way."

"I'm sure you will, Mike," replied Pippa, playing along. "It was silly of me, wasn't it?"

"Extremely."

It was then that Pippa noticed up they were well into Cairo, but not turning for Roda Island and the hotel. They were going a completely unknown route.

"Where are we going?" He didn't answer. She tried again and there was an uneasy feeling in the pit of her stomach. "Mike, where are we? You're supposed to be taking me to Dad. That was the arrangement."

"Well, the arrangements have changed." His voice was icy cool. "You'll just have to make the best of it. I can't risk you opening your mouth just now."

"Let me out," Pippa shouted. He took no notice. They were driving very fast and the roads were narrowing and less well lit. "Mike, be sensible. I don't want to go where you're going. I want to go to the hotel."

"I'm sorry, but it's out of the question. And stop behaving like a little fool. If you jump out, you'll break your neck." Mike was still accelerating and Pippa could do was protest wildly as he swung the jeep into the densely-populated streets of the poorest part of Cairo.

Several times, swarthy passers-by stared impassively at the beautiful, fair-haired girl knocking for help on the vehicle's windows as it slowed down to negotiate the narrow streets, but no-one appeared to try and help her. Everyone just ignored her shouting and frantic gestures as if they were nothing.

Soon, Pippa realised that wherever she was, it wasn't in the guide books. The lights of the city were receding with every second that passed. There were only glimmers of light now on either side of the jeep, from strange, low buildings outlined against the orange-neon sky glow of distant street lights. It was as dark as death.

They were on Cairo's fringes, and even the lights of a car that was behind them vanished. Pippa had given up pulling at Mike's jacket and trying to stop him. He had hurled her aside twice and she was afraid they might crash. She sat in frightened silence, trying to use her brain. He was abducting her. He was crazy. She had to be clever if she was going to get away from him. He'd certainly gone mad. When he stopped, she might be able to give him the slip. But where was she? How would she get away?

Finally, the jeep bumped to a stop outside a menacing, dark building; its entrance a yawning mouth in the vehicle's lights. It was the end of the road.

"What is this place? Where are we?"

Mike didn't answer as he pulled the key from the ignition.

It was then she attempted to wrench open the passenger door. But he caught her by the arm, his fingers digging brutally into her flesh. Then he was dragging her *across* to his seat, squashing her legs against the dashboard, trapping them. She shouted in pain, but he took no notice and kept on pulling her.

"No, no, you're hurting me," screamed Pippa. "Stop! Stop, Mike! Where are you taking me? Stop it, Mike, while you have the chance."

"Get out," he said. She disengaged her bare legs, grimacing as she grazed them. She had torn her dress as well. Then he was wrenching her out of the driver's side. She stumbled at his force and fell on the ground. He dragged her up in what seemed to be a lane and pulled her towards that sinister entrance.

She could see it was made of stone. And the opening was narrow and rectangular. What did it remind her of? The pyramid. Then she realised with utter shock it *was* the entrance to a tomb. And they were going in.

She knew where she was. Rik had mentioned it a long time ago. The City of the Dead. A horrible place, where the poorest in the population dragged out their existence.

An enormous area of eerie cemeteries, the only place where the wandering homeless of Cairo could find a place to sleep. *Sarcophagi. The very word frightened her. Flesh-eaters. Oh, Rik*, she cried to herself, as Mike Nash dragged her inside. He was like a dead man, saying nothing, feeling nothing for her. *Rik, Rik, why didn't I let you know what he said about you and Mia? Then I wouldn't have been here.*

Pippa was crying as he pulled her deep into the musty darkness, their echoing, stumbling feet striking the stones. And, in the distance, she could see flashing lights coming towards them. Torches. What was going to happen to her? Her mouth was dry...

Pippa had promised herself she'd be brave, but now she was seriously afraid. She couldn't bear the thought of being in the dark with him. Them? Were they going to kill her? Mike had surely gone mad.

"Let me go," she tried again, struggling.

"Shut your mouth!" he shouted back. "I've too much to lose." Next minute, the torches were shining in their faces and, after that first blinding moment, when Pippa's eyes accustomed to the dark, she glimpsed Mike's face and realised, to her horror, that whoever his accomplices were, Mike was as terrified of them as she was.

* * *

The Mercedes which had been following the jeep at a distance all the way into the City of the Dead, slid to a halt. The handsome, dark young man at the wheel looked drawn and his lips were set in a grim line. It had been quite a problem keeping up with the jeep in all those narrow streets.

The pretty Egyptian woman beside him had her mouth close to the two-way transmitter, relaying instructions.

"Over and out." Mia Gabal turned to the driver and smiled. "Don't worry, Rik," she said, putting the receiver back and patting his arm. "We know where she is now and, remember, everything is still going according to plan."

* * *

CHAPTER 11

Pippa opened her eyes and, from her mattress in the corner, stared around her prison. No, it was not a dream. She was inside a tomb. And there was a light shining through the open grating in the door. A bright light full of dusty particles, but a light. She fought off the claustrophobic feelings she'd had last night when they'd thrown her in there with only a torch.

The events of her capture crowded and jostled into her consciousness. Mike had abducted her. He and two other hooded and robed men had dumped her on a mattress, thrown her in a sleeping bag and left her. But she was still alive, and she had a proper light now.

Pippa ran to the heavy, barred door with the grating in it, which was the only opening in her cell. She had to stand on tiptoe to look through. The abrasions on her leg hurt and she was stiff and sore. She realised there was no use shouting for help. She was below ground level and the grating looked out on to a corridor, cut out of rough stone. But there was a lighted gaz lantern in a recess. What if they put it out? She panicked then. She couldn't bear the thought and began to bang her small fists against the door.

"Let me out, damn you. Let me out."

But no-one came. Pippa drew back wearily and went and sat on the mattress. What was going to happen? Why was Mike doing this? What had she done? She buried her head in her hands, thinking how worried her father would be, how somebody must miss her very, very soon.

A few minutes later, she was attempting to pull herself together, going over the events after Mike had forcibly dragged her out of the vehicle and into the darkness. Where was she? The City of the Dead was to the east of Cairo. Would anyone ever think of looking for her there? The city was enormous, and there would be no leads as to her whereabouts. She could be here for years. They might think she'd gone back to England. Negative thoughts engulfed her.

She shook her head then put it in her hands and tried to think. It was no good giving up. The police would comb every part of the city. Her father was an important man.

She had to fight off the hopeless feelings which kept rising up in her throat, choking her. She was a psychologist. She had to be stronger than this. What had the hostages in Beirut done? They'd survived for years.

Was she a hostage?

Mike had said nothing. Neither had the two men. She suspected they were Egyptians. They'd come back half an hour later. That was when she thought they were going to kill her. They were the same men, hooded so she couldn't recognise them, but they'd got rid of their robes and were wearing European clothes. They stood there, arguing, flashing their torches in her face until she was dizzy.

But they hadn't touched her and, when they'd gone, she'd collapsed exhausted on the mattress with only the torch for light. She was afraid to keep it on all night as the battery would soon become exhausted. She only used it to see the time.

She had worn herself out banging on the door and begging them to let her go, but they'd ignored her. Later, one of them brought her a plate of food which she didn't touch. They had left her finally and she'd fallen asleep. But now she had the shaft of light from the gaz lantern.

* * *

Her watch said it was nearly ten in the morning. Her palms were sore from the exertion of drumming on the door and her throat hoarse from yelling. She felt light-headed. She'd also been crying constantly, which wasn't like her. She felt drained and broken.

Some time later, Pippa raised her head dully as the key turned in the lock. All kinds of thoughts went through her mind as the door opened. She looked up to see Mike's face.

She flew at him. "How dare you? How dare you?" She was sobbing and drumming her hands against his chest. He caught hold of her wrists hard.

"Stop it," he yelled and slapped her face with a force that sent her reeling. Shocked into silence, Pippa let go.

"That's better. Calm down. No-one's going to do anything to you. Just be quiet." He was looking behind him. "I mean it," he whispered. "Either you stay quiet or I can't be responsible. It isn't up to me any more. Do you understand?"

"I don't understand anything," she cried. "What are you doing? Why am I here in this horrible place?"

"It's only for a short time, until . . ." He hesitated. She knew he was as frightened as she was.

"Tell me, Mike, tell me," she said, gritting her teeth and trying to calm down. Perspiration and tears were running down her dirty face and she brushed them away with equally grimy hands. "How could you do this to me - after London and . . ."

"I didn't want any of this to happen, Pippa. But you know too much. And Ahmed . . ."

"What do you mean? What does Ahmed have to do with this?"

"I mean Ahmed had it in for you. You found the stuff. You're right. He wanted you to. He knew they'd get you if you found it. "

"Who, Mike? Who are *they*?"

"Never mind who they are. Just believe me when I say they're not very nice people to deal with." Mike's face was white.

"What are you into, Mike?" She was terrified now. "You're scared as well. Why did you try to put the blame on Rik and Mia? Why did you do it?"

"Don't ask me." He stood with his back to her, facing the wall.

"When are they going to let me go?"

"When they get the stuff out." He spoke quietly.

"And you were the one who stole it for them? It wasn't Rik or Mia. It was you. You're selling treasures, aren't you? Selling out on Dad and the project. The money. How could you do it?"

"You don't understand anything. If it wasn't for me, they'd have got rid of you by now. So shut up."

She gasped at the violence in his tone. He turned and the look on his face was despairing and desperate. It was then she knew it was no use appealing to him; no use relying on their past relationship. There was no way

131

Mike was going to let her go. She sat down quietly and let her long hair fall over her shoulders.

"I don't understand," she said. "I could beg you to tell me, but I can see it would be no use. What are they going to do with me?"

"They promised me they'd let you go after, that's all I know," he said. "I came to tell you that. I can tell you nothing else." He turned to leave. She caught hold of his arm again and he tried to disengage it.

"Mike, stop, listen. Is it too late for us to get away? We could go to the police. Together? We could explain everything. They could help you."

"Good try, Pippa, but it's no use. You just sit tight and keep quiet. Or it'll be too late. Remember what nearly happened to your dad? And the falling logs? Keep that in your mind and do as you're told." He was backing away, the light silhouetting his angular frame. A moment later, he'd be gone and she'd be alone again.

He moved very quickly and the door thudded shut behind him. She breathed in deeply just to stop herself screaming. She knew she'd have to play this game, but would they keep their promise? Who were they? What were they? Whoever they were, they'd frightened Mike into complete submission.

Pippa shivered with fear, wrapping her arms around her trembling frame. There was nothing she could do, only sit and pray someone would come and get her out of her deep and already stifling prison.

* * *

The blazing day outside dragged on to night. The men on guard in those narrow alleyways which led to Pippa's

132

prison, looked in through the grating frequently on their prisoner who lay dejected on her mattress. They were satisfied because she was quiet now.

Outside, under the cover of darkness, an athletic figure, dressed in black combat gear dived into the dark entrance of the mausoleum. And then another... And another...

Where the stone corridor widened out into a junction cut into the rock, one of Pippa's guards lighted the other's cigarette from his. As the men bent their heads together, they felt one jarring shock. The next moment, they were lying unconscious.

Then the special armed police squad continued sneaking and spreading throughout the complex, surprising and finishing off the other guards. It was only when they reached the heart of the operations taking place in that complicated underground network, they were forced to open fire.

Pippa put her hands over her ears at the sound of rapid automatic gun fire. What was happening? Would she be next? She shrank into a corner of the room, her wide eyes watching the grating in the locked door. She could hear the key moving in the lock. This was it. They were going to kill her.

The noise in her throat strangled itself. Mike had told her to keep quiet. She had to. The door burst open. She raised her head, screwed up her face, and found herself looking straight into the blunt nose of an automatic pistol.

This was it. She was going to die.

"Please, please don't shoot," she screamed, blinded by the light. "I haven't done anything. Please, listen to me, please."

And then, in that critical split second, she heard a

familiar voice. "Pippa, thank God. Pippa, are you all right?" And she was in Rik Fenton's arms being cradled close. "Oh, Pippa, I was so frightened. I didn't know what they'd do to you. My love, you're safe now, don't worry."

She almost fainted with shock and relief. Then he was pushing the hair back from her tear-stained face. "Have they hurt you, have they?"

She clung to him terrified that he would leave her alone. "No," she sobbed, "no, Rik. Oh, Rik, I'm so glad to see you. Oh, Rik."

"Shush, darling," he said, holding her close, "you're all right now. I've got you. You're all right." And he was kissing her, holding her shaking body tight.

A few moments later, escorted by two burly members of the special police force, Pippa was half-carried through the stone passageways of the complex towards the yawning mouth of the mausoleum.

Outside, the narrow thoroughfare was no longer dark and deserted. The flashing lights of a waiting ambulance and a number of police car sirens were filling the area with sound and brilliance. Closing her eyes in utter relief, poor, exhausted Pippa was loaded into the ambulance.

Next moment, the lithe, black-clothed figure of Rik Fenton was jumping in behind her and the vehicle was screaming on its way towards the neon lights of the more fashionable quarter of Egypt's capital city.

* * *

Rik Fenton knocked on the door of Room 57 of Cairo Police Headquarters. Then, at the sound of a female voice, led Pippa into the room.

It was exactly ten hours after her rescue. She'd been

taken to the University Hospital, checked over and released after an emotional re-union with her father and a very good rest. Rik had refused to say much about the raid, just told her to concentrate on getting herself over her ordeal. He added that it was the job of the police to do all the explaining.

There, in the room, seated behind an imposing desk, was a dark-eyed woman of about thirty-five, her glasses perched upon her hair and a warm smile on her face. Mia Gabal. And she was jumping to her feet and hurrying round to meet them.

"Mia!" Pippa cried, looking from her to Rik. He was grinning too. "What are you doing here?"

"I work here - for my sins," the Egyptian said. She kissed Pippa on both cheeks, then Pippa turned to Rik and he kissed her as well.

"I'm afraid we've been holding out on you, Pippa," Rik said. "Mia's a policewoman." Pippa looked from one to the other. She could hardly take it in.

"I thought you were an archaeologist," she said. "I don't understand."

"Oh, I am. An amateur one. It was a necessary pretence. And . . ." she put her arm round Pippa, ". . . I'm really sorry things got so hot. But we had no choice."

"Will somebody please explain?" Pippa said wearily. She was still too exhausted to concentrate.

"Here, take a pew," Rik replied, rushing to fetch her a chair. "Pippa, you look absolutely worn out."

"I am. All I seem to want to do is sleep, but I'm not going to until somebody tells me what's been going on." How many times had she said that since she landed in Cairo?

Mia sat down again and Rik perched himself on the

edge of her desk. Pippa thought what a magnificent-looking couple they made, so self-confident and supremely assertive.

"Pippa," Mia said, turning over some papers in front of her, "as you see and as you've heard from us both, I am no archaeologist. In fact, I'm a police inspector. I have been working undercover with special forces here in Cairo. I do have a background in archaeology, though. That's why I was attached to your father's project as soon as there was some suspicion of theft."

"You didn't suspect Dad, surely?" Pippa cried.

"No, of course not. He's a man of great integrity and well-known here. However, his assistant was not."

Pippa frowned sadly, shaking her head. "Mike?"

"Yes, Pippa, and I'm sorry."

"Don't be. Mike has meant nothing to me for a long time. It was different in London but, here, in Egypt, he was like a stranger. And, after what he did to me just now, how do you think I feel?" She could hear the anger in her own voice about being treated like that.

There was a strange look on Rik's face, as if he was more than interested in what Pippa had just said. The same kind of look he'd had when he'd cradled her in his arms and half-carried her out of that horrible place. But, maybe it had been just relief she was safe.

Or was it?

He smiled at her.

"That's good news," Mia said. "The things I'm about to tell you will be less painful." She exchanged glances with Rik. "You know, of course, that Mike Nash joined your father's team after he'd been working for several years in South America?"

"Yes. I know that."

"I'm afraid that while Mike was over in Colombia he became involved in a very dangerous game. As an ambitious, young man he made several unwise deals with local drug dealers, just so he could have the chance to open up a new site which he felt was of tremendous importance. He also developed another very dangerous habit - he became an addict."

"Mike? A drug addict?" She could hardly believe it, but that could explain his strange behaviour, the way he'd been in London, the sudden unpredictable changes of mood, and his final disastrous change of character in Egypt.

"There really wasn't a lot anyone could do for Mike by the time he joined your father's team in Cairo," Mia said quietly. "It is quite easy to understand what happened. He was under enormous pressure through his Colombian connections and his inability to kick his habit. They used him quite brilliantly. Their network is very big in Cairo. Through Mike they had a chance to expand even further and he had the means to pay, at last, for his addiction."

Mia sat back in her chair, her eyes watching Pippa closely. "We were first on his tail when Rik here discovered the objects going missing. If it hadn't been for Rik, we would never have broken the ring, nor have recovered the main bulk of the stolen artefacts. Not only from your father's dig, but from many other sources.

"Rik smelled a rat from the first, and he didn't hesitate in doing something about it. He came to us straight away, and managed to keep the information away from your father, as he knew his health was beginning to break down. Yes, Rik has been a tower of strength to all of us."

Mia Gabal smiled at Rik who smiled back, shaking his head.

"To both of you," Pippa remarked flatly.

"No," Rik said, getting off the desk, "Pippa - I don't know quite how to say this, but what Mia means is . . ."

"You've no need to explain anything," Pippa said. It was most embarrassing. She didn't want to hear about their affair. In any case, what was it to do with her?

"Let me, Rik," Mia said. "I didn't want to tell you just like this, Pippa, but what Rik means is that I . . . your father and I . . ."

"My father and you?" Pippa was confused. "What about Dad?"

Mia cleared her throat and shuffled the papers, looking not at all like a practised police inspector. "What I'm trying to say is . . . that over the last few months, your father and I have become extremely good friends." Pippa was staring at Mia. "That we . . ." Mia Gabal was clasping and unclasping her hands, breathing in deeply. "Haven't you noticed, Pippa? I'm in love with your father."

"Oh," Pippa said. *"You and my father are in love?"*

"I thought you were supposed to be a psychologist," Rik said quietly, looking from Pippa towards Mia's embarrassed face. "Can't you make this any easier for her, Pippa?"

"Do you mind terribly?" Mia asked. "John wanted to tell you ages ago but I wouldn't let him. I couldn't spring that on you with the memories of your mother still fresh in your mind."

"Mia, oh, Mia," Pippa cried, jumping up from the chair. Her tiredness seemed to have suddenly disappeared. "Mind? Of course I don't mind. I'm so happy for you."

"You are?" Rik said. "Great!" He was looking at both women in a puzzled way.

"Did you think I wouldn't be?" Pippa asked.

138

"Frankly, yes, I did," she admitted softly. "We both did."

"How typical of Dad," Pippa said to Mia. "I was surprised, that's all. It's come as a shock."

"That's why I didn't say anything before. Especially when John was so ill. I wanted to," Mia added.

"I understand completely," Pippa said, sitting down again. She couldn't believe how happy she felt. Mia and Dad. In love. So Rik . . . She looked up at him. "Thank you, Rik, for saving my life. *Twice.*" Now he was the one who looked embarrassed.

"Well, that's over," Mia said, "and I can't wait to have a long, long talk with you. I just can't wait, but I have to. Back to the point." She turned to her desk, walked round and sat down.

Pippa felt quite dizzy now as if a weight had been lifted from her.

"About Rik," she began.

"Yes?" Pippa said, smiling.

"He's supported your father all the way through - and me. I apologise that we couldn't tell you what was going on, but it was far too dangerous. We had to take that risk and I'm so sorry about what you've had to put up with. It must have been awful." Mia Gabal laid a sympathetic hand on Pippa's arm. "But we were watching you and Mike very closely."

"That's why you offered to drive me to the site, wasn't it?" All Pippa could think of was that Rik and Mia were only good friends.

"Of course. That's why we were always around. We wanted to make sure nothing would happen to you. But we hadn't reckoned on Ahmed's viciousness. And he had also been paid very well by the dealers."

A thought suddenly came to Pippa. "How did Dad fall? Was it Mike? Or Ahmed?"

"We're not sure, but we'll find out. I prefer to think it was Ahmed," Mia said. "Whether Mike Nash would stoop to attempted murder . . ."

"He said that he made them promise to free me," Pippa replied quickly. "That's after they got the treasures away of course. He seemed pretty desperate himself."

"Ahmed certainly engineered the log episode," Rik said. "He's a nasty little customer. Still, we'll see how he likes it in jail."

"But what about Mike? What will happen to him? Will he be sent to prison, too?" she asked.

Pippa knew the punishment for Mike's crimes were harsh in Egypt.

"That's for the courts here to decide," Mia said crisply, "but I don't think they'll be lenient."

"You're not worrying about him, I hope," Rik said determinedly. "He deserves all he gets, Pippa. Especially after what he put you through."

"Anyone does who deals with drugs," Mia added seriously.

Pippa nodded, but she still felt sad about it all. Mike's whole life - it was such a terrible waste.

She sighed. "No, I'm not worrying. I don't know what's the matter with me. I suppose I'm really tired. I admit it was an awful experience. I was terrified not knowing what was going to happen. I never thought I'd be so scared." She shivered.

Rik put out his hand and closed it over hers. She liked the feel of his strong, warm fingers. She responded with a slight pressure.

"I'd like to get back to the hotel as quickly as possible. But what about Dad? Does he know all this?"

"He knew quite a bit before but, like us, he was bound to say nothing. One thing I can tell you - he's going to be so relieved."

"Just as I was about giving you my news." Mia got up suddenly. She came round the desk, put her arms round Pippa and hugged her close. "You do look worn out. You should go back now and rest."

"Come on, Pippa," Rik said, stepping forward. He still looked as indestructible as the day he'd climbed the pyramid with her, and he couldn't have had any sleep. "I'll take you back. Are you coming?" he asked Mia.

She shook her head, her eyes gleaming behind her spectacles. "No, not just now. You two go along. But tell John I'll be over to see him later. And take care - both of you."

Pippa felt Rik's arm about her shoulders and, with an imperceptible sigh of relief, she let Rik lead her to the office door. "Goodbye, Mia," she said warmly, "and thank you."

"It was my pleasure," the older woman said. Mia Gabal was still smiling as she heard their feet echoing along the corridor. Then she bent over the papers on her desk and started working.

* * *

Firmly, Rik closed the door of Pippa's room at the Hotel Saladin. Her father was spending a couple of nights at the dig now he knew Pippa was safe.

"Alone at last," he said, holding out his arms.

Pippa stepped into them and nestled her head into the

141

hollow of his shoulder. She shivered with pleasure as he stroked her hair gently.

"You're very quiet," he murmured.

She let him go on, soothing her aching body, but every nerve in hers was thrilling to his touch. Then she lifted her head. "All I want to do is just feel your hands doing this," she said, knowing he couldn't help but recognise the open invitation in both her words and her eyes.

She closed the lids as his lips moved down from her forehead and on to her lips. His tongue searched her mouth urgently, and all the need for closeness she'd dreamed of since she came to Egypt was contained in that one, deep, wonderful kiss.

"Darling," he murmured, and Pippa could feel his athlete's body harden against hers. She caught her breath in pleasure.

"Rik," she breathed, "I'm so glad that . . . that you and Mia . . ."

"Don't talk," he commanded, "just let me hold you."

Suddenly, they were staring into each other's eyes and his dark and smouldering look made her feel quite dizzily unreal. She hardly knew what she was doing when he lifted her off her feet and carried her easily over to the bed.

"You're not too tired, are you?" he asked softly as he leaned over her.

"What do you think?" she smiled, putting up her hands and beginning to unbutton his shirt. She could see his heart beating wildly under the skin so, drawing him right down towards her, Pippa began to caress him too. All her worries about him and Mia had disappeared; her fears for the future were receding, and her whole being was suddenly engulfed with love for Rik . . . and only Rik.

142

He was smiling with delight as he arched his back and began to kiss her all over. Pippa lay, allowing the delightful tingles of passion course through her body as he kissed every intimate and secret spot she hardly knew she possessed, bringing with his caresses a mad excitement she had never experienced before.

And then, in the midst of their wild lovemaking, her whole body was responding, carrying them both away into another world, where Pippa's head was full of stormy and tempestuous sands as she rode with her lover over the edge of ecstasy.

All she could remember of that marvellous moment of intimacy was her cry of delight and relief and, afterwards, the safe feeling that their tired, but satisfied bodies could really rest at last.

As she drifted off into happy sleep, she remembered thinking that to be in Cairo with Rik was the loveliest place in the world.

* * *

CHAPTER 12

Pippa gazed at the armadas of feluccas drifting slowly down the Nile, their billowing sails like flimsy butterfly wings, their masts dipping gracefully towards the water.

She and Rik were standing on the fertile fringe of the great river again. They had driven over from the site. As Pippa gazed across the shimmering water, she was thinking about her first night in Egypt when she'd stared at the same view with Mia and Mike.

It seemed a very long time ago and, now, her eventful holiday in Egypt was coming to an end. Such a lot had happened since she last looked at this view. "It's so lovely," she murmured, thinking how much more beautiful it was, enjoying it with Rik.

Rik glanced down at Pippa, his eyes shining with love. "So are you." Her attention never strayed from the view before her.

"Thank you. You're not bad yourself," she answered mischievously. It was wonderful just being allowed to be oneself, not having to pretend any more.

"And thank *you*. There's nothing I like more than being complimented by beautiful women." He was in a playful mood too. How had she ever thought Rik arrogant? He was just Rik. They were getting to know each other very well. She stopped looking at the view and up at him. His smooth, tanned skin had a golden hue and his eyes and mouth looked lazy and sweet. She lifted a finger playfully and traced the lines of his mouth. He snapped at her and she jumped.

"What are you doing?"

"I'm being a Nile crocodile," he grinned.

"No," she joked, "I think you look more like Rameses II than a croc. It's the nose."

"Don't be silly," he said. "Young King Tut. Now there was a good-looking fellow." They stared at the view companionably.

"I shall miss Egypt," she said, suddenly serious. "Even the heat." She brushed back her damp hair. "I think it's a magical place. It kind of grows on you."

"Why should you?" he asked suddenly.

She turned at the question. "I beg your pardon?"

"Miss it," Rik repeated. "You don't have to."

She frowned, her mind filling with reasons for her return to England; her work, her friends, all the things she had left behind. She'd been here for almost six weeks and had nearly used up her whole year's leave.

"Well, I have to go back to London one day soon, or I shan't have a job any more. The trust will be advertising for a new psychologist." She knew she wasn't looking forward to it.

"Let them," Rik said.

Pippa's heart thumped. "What do you mean?"

"I mean I don't want you to go. I mean I want you to stay here, with me." His dark, piercing eyes were searching her face.

"And what would I do?" She waited breathlessly, begging inside for the question she wanted to hear more than anything in the world.

He stretched out his strong, comforting arms and drew her to him. She could feel his heart beating rapidly under the thin shirt he wore. Her heart's rhythm was just as fast.

"You could marry me?"

She closed her eyes in relief, his warm skin burning against hers. Then she laid her head on his chest and snuggled into him. She didn't have to think about it. A moment later, she raised her head and replied simply, "Okay, I will."

She felt an impulse like an electric current run through her. He quivered as if he felt it, too. Then his mouth sought her lips, its gentle touch deepening with the passion they seemed to be experiencing all the time they were together.

They couldn't keep their hands off each other. It would have been death to go back to London and leave him. But, as usual, with Pippa, it was all or nothing. And they were deeply in love.

When they broke apart, dizzy, after that wonderful kiss, they walked back to the jeep hand in hand. Soon they were bumping over the dunes and along the makeshift road to the site.

A lazy, satisfied smile played about Rik's lips as he manoeuvred the vehicle skilfully. "Shall we tell your father and Mia now?" he asked.

"Why not?" she said, returning his smile.

"Looks like another sandstorm on the way," he said, peering through the windscreen. "But, this time, it can't hurt us. Everything's in place."

It was - in all senses of the word.

On the horizon, the sand was whirling and stirring itself into a tempestuous cloud, its power greater than any other in the desert.

"It's been doing that for ever, Rik," she murmured.

"The sands of time, eh?" he replied. "But it's our time now, Pippa. It won't shift us, will it?" She shook her head.

Together, they watched the strong wind blow along the margin of the sands, breaking them apart, but she and Rik took their strength from one another.

"Well, Pippa," Rik said, looking across at her in a comfortable kind of way, "it'll take more than the sand-devil to part us. Take it from me. And I'm always right."

She could have argued with him as she had argued so many times before, but today she chose not to. Today she would agree with him. Why spoil the most beautiful day in her life?

"For once I think you might be," Pippa smiled.

Suddenly, he braked and, leaning over, began to kiss her again and again. When she got her breath back, she added mischievously, "But only this once."

Rik Fenton smiled wickedly and, patting her gently on the knee, drove the dusty jeep off into the approaching sandstorm.

THE END

Also available in the

MYSTERIES OF THE HEART

series

Forever Yours - Helen McCabe
After the Rain - Aisling Byrne
Tides of Love - Helen McCabe

Helen McCabe

Forever Yours

Lorne is working happily in Lanzarote, until her past, in the shape of Shane Westonman shows up.
What was the intriguing secret she'd been hiding?

ISBN 0-9525404-8-7

AISLING BYRNE

AFTER THE RAIN

Should ex-Army officer Alison trust Richard? What was the secret he was keeping from her? Could the Army be to blame again?

ISBN 0-9525404-7-9

Helen McCabe

Tides of Love

Could Fran's childhood sweetheart, Declan O'Neill, have been responsible for her father's mysterious death at sea? One stormy night, Fran is prepared to risk everything to find out. Even her own life, and that of the man she loves.

ISBN 0-9525404-2-8

**Also available now from Peacock Publishing Ltd
in the SPLENDOUR series**

Two for a Lie - Helen McCabe
Eve's Daughter - Michael Taylor
Raven's Mill - Helen McCabe

Forthcoming Title

A Driving Passion - Michael Taylor

Two for a Lie

Helen McCabe

'An epic saga blending historical fact, fiction and fantasy - a stunning read. I couldn't put it down!'
Susan Sallis

Mary Willcocks, aged eighteen, is returning home across the moor when she is waylaid and almost raped by the brutal Humphrey Moon, the wild young son of her former master. She is saved by her hero, Jem Farr, the half-French ward of the local squire. And Mary's love remains his throughout the many tragedies she has to face before her dreams come true.

Passion, intrigue, murder and revenge are the ingredients of this rich adventure set in the early 1800s. How Mary, the servant girl was transformed into the exotic PRINCESS CARABOO has puzzled scholars and her admirers for two hundred years. At last, her secrets are revealed in *Two for a Lie,* which is itself based on a dream as rich as Mary's own.

'*Two for a Lie* is more than a novel. Helen McCabe is a master storyteller with the unique gift of making history come alive in the astonishing adventures of her heroine. When I came away, I had a firsthand knowledge of early nineteenth-century life, and also found myself missing Mary . . .'
Shahrukh Husain

ISBN 0-9525404-0-1

A DRIVING PASSION

Michael Taylor

Lovely Henzey Kite is wary of allowing herself to fall in love again after her first heady affair with prosperous man-about-town, Billy Witts. But men find her beauty and her talent as an artist irresistible. Then, deeply drawn to handsome engineer Will Parish, a widower, Henzey finds another man vying for her love; wealthy motor manufacturer Dudley Worthington, a married man. Only Dudley is aware of the astonishing links between these three men; links that are enough to turn all their lives upside-down. . .

Set within the external glamour and internal graft of the burgeoning West Midlands' motor industry in the 20s and 30s, *A Driving Passion* is a spellbinding saga of obsession, agonising love and restless guilt.

A sequel to *Eve's Daughter*, this compulsive tale confirms Michael Taylor as one of the few male writers able to achieve a warm empathy with the heroine.

Due out Spring 1998

ISBN 0-9525404-6-0

All Peacock books are available at your local bookshop. In case of difficulty, they can be obtained from:

Littlehampton Book Services Ltd.,
10-14 Eldon Way
Lineside Industrial Estate
Littlehampton
West Sussex BN17 7HE
United Kingdom

Direct Sales Line:
01903 736736 (fax no. 01903 730828)
International +44 1903 736736 (International fax +44 1903 730828)
Please quote the title you require, author, ISBN, and credit card number - Visa/MasterCard.

Card No._____

Expiry Date _____

Signature_____

Peacock Publishing Ltd. reserves the right to charge new retail prices, if necessary, which may differ from those shown.

Title_____ Quantity_____

Author_____ISBN_____

Address to which book(s) to be forwarded:

Name_____

Address_____

_____

Please allow 28 days for delivery